WYRD JUSTICE-

WEEKENDS IN

DYSTOPIA

By Luna Q'otu

Wyrd Justice- Weekends in Dystopia by Luna Q'otu

This compilation of stories is dedicated to my Sisterchicks.

Brave, funny, so very powerful; we every one of us quietly hold the universe together for our families and ourselves, an intermingling web of humanity we casually refer to as community.

Never let anyone tell you that you are less than magnificent.

Never let anyone limit your capacity for greatness.

Those who conspire to keep you down only do so because they lack the character and strength to rise.

Always remember fighting fire with fire only burns the world faster.

We're better than that.

Stay wild, stay free, stay grounded and fly.

Namaste.

Wyrd Justice- Weekends in Dystopia by Luna Q'otu

"...remember the ladies, and be more generous and favorable to them than your ancestors.

Do not put such unlimited power into the hands of the Husbands.

Remember all Men would be tyrants if they could.

If particular care and attention is not paid to the Ladies we are determined to foment a Rebellion, and will not hold ourselves bound by any Laws in which we have no voice, or Representation."

-Abigail Adams

Wyrd Justice- Weekends in Dystopia by Luna Q'otu

<u>Introduction</u>

The end is near, but so then is the beginning.

This story is told in six parts, and while they are in order, they are not in the same timeframe.

Each one encompasses only a few days, hence the title, *'Weekends in Dystopia'*.

The forces in play are already set in motion as of my writing this- only some very tiny alterations would be necessary to tip the future in the direction as written.

There could be several years between occurrences…or several months.

My heroine is beautiful, flawed, sexy, frail and powerful. Just like all women.

She has possibly an unusual advantage- hence the title, *'Wyrd Justice'*- but considering the average human taps into only a tiny fraction of their own mind, who knows what we might all be capable of, if only we were to believe in ourselves more, and what we are *supposed* to believe less.

Preface

Death is funny.

Tom Devine, aged 40, gazed calmly into serious brown eyes flecked with green that were locked unblinkingly onto his.

He was still tanned; deceivingly healthy-looking except for the gauntness of flesh on his formerly strong frame and the hollowing under his eyes as everything seemed to shrink and suck inward in a futile attempt to condense whatever life was left in him into a compact and strong chunk of carbon-based mammal.

He didn't have too many regrets, even though he was getting taken out of the game barely at half-time. He'd seen most all of the world he wanted to, and found the universe's most perfect woman who by some miracle fell in love with him.

His main regret, of course, was that he'd never see his daughter as a grown woman, or even a toddler. Never see the finished product that the gorgeous brown eyes were the beginning of.

But regrets were for people who had time to spare on such things, and he was not one of those.

So he held her tiny body on his chest and looked into her eyes.

He worried, of course.

Tom knew that Janet would do whatever she needed to do to raise their daughter safely. He had no doubt in his mind that little Fate could not ask for better hands to be in than the strong, gentle hands of her mother.

But the world was getting so sideways. He and Janet had talked long and seriously about the changes that were coming to their country- what it would look like for their daughter and how they'd need to prepare her for the almost constant turmoil they saw ahead.

He trusted Janet. He had to trust in Fate to find her way through it. Something told him that she had it in her to not just survive, but to be a part of helping others as well.

She *was* her mother's daughter.

Tom' eyelids grew heavy and he sighed and closed his eyes.

Even after his eyes closed he could see his daughter's eyes in his mind.

Life is funny.

Only a month old, she stared seriously into her father's green eyes flecked with brown.

She knew him by sight, by sound, by smell, by touch. Knew she was part of him.

While her mother was up and around and constantly doing something in a never-ending flurry of frustrated helpless activity, her father seemed never to leave the bed, so that's where little Fate spent most of her time- snuggled on his chest.

She watched as his eyes closed in exhaustion and laid her head down, closing her eyes as well.

For the previous thirty days, she'd gone to sleep with the sound of his heart echoing in her head and absorbed through her skin.

She drifted off to sleep to the rhythmic beating, stirring slightly as it slowed, waking as is skipped once or twice.

When it stopped, she began to cry and her mother rushed into the room, scooped her up and they cried together.

Fate fell asleep to the sound of her mother's heartbeat and the scent of her Black Orchid perfume.

BOOK ONE-

HAMMERED!

POUNDING IT HOME FOR LIBERTY

Prologue

Fumbling in the darkened smoke-filled guts of what used to be this tiny corner of civilization, Butch instinctively found what he was looking for; years of familiarity, use and muscle memory served him well and his hand closed gently yet urgently around what he needed most.

Closing his eyes and focusing inward, Butch let his fingers play along the rock-hard smoothness, hesitating just a moment before his fingertips stroked over the head and he sighed; excitement an electrical current from his fingers to his brain and pulsing back down through his torso.

In his mind's eye he could see her, hear her, feel her, smell her. The scent of leather and sunshine and Black Orchid filled his head intoxicatingly.

He knew then that he would survive.

His eyes opened and he smiled, gazing lovingly down at the source of his pleasure and his assurance in his skills- seeming to glow with an almost living quality lay his ticket out of here- his beloved Wilton 20.

When he had purchased it, it had seemed like overkill. Thirty six inches long, well over twenty pounds, it boasted a vulcanized rubber and tempered steel rod handle and an enormous seven inch head.

That baby would bust through anything without hesitation and keep going all day long- and all night if necessary.

Grinning in testosterone-filled anticipation in spite of the long odds facing him, Butch grabbed ahold of his perfect tool in both hands tightly and commenced to pounding.

Chapter One- Attraction

They met at the Range.

He was just doing a little routine practice- keeping his edge even though he was a master already, and it showed...oh, it showed.

The friendly chatter turned to hushed murmurs when his truck drove across the dusty meadow because no one ever knew just what new 'toy' he'd brought to tinker with on any given day. The truck was metallic black and he kept it spotless.

A gleaming Ford F350 King Ranch 4D Crew Cab, Butch had taken this already awesome display of manliness and pushed it as far to the limit as possible. Wrangler MT/R's with Kevlar ensured that this vehicle would stop for no one and nothing would get in its way. From the chrome American Eagle hood ornament to the Old Glory Flag decal in the back window to the gleaming silver 'truck nuts' swaying hypnotically from the trailer hitch, the truck was a sight to behold.

 The man and truck seemed as one- each matching the other's physical perfection and strength. The sign on the side of the truck seemed redundant since there could be no doubt who *this* truck belonged to.

Steven Owen "Butch" Butcher

"Doin' it Right the First Time"

(xxx)574-TDOG

The big diesel engine rumbled, coughed, and was still; you could hear the breeze from a dropping pin as the door swung open. When Butch had first bought his truck, he had practiced in his driveway until he could effortlessly appear to not just hop out of the big vehicle, but seem to *saunter* out.

Pretending not to be aware of the many eyes riveted to the back of his head, Butch whistled softly and made his way to the big locked box bolted into the back of his truck.

He was dressed to match his truck- all in black from head to toes. While he didn't wear a hat (he was too proud of his perfect mane of raven hair untouched by silver even though he was pushing 50), he did hide his ice blue eyes behind Ray Ban Wayfarer 622's with rubber frames and lenses dark enough to be opaque. His brushed cotton Armani shirt was impeccably cut; deceptively simple. His classic Levi jeans were black-on-black dark and fit like the proverbial glove, and his Luchesse American Alligator Belly Bias Cut boots gleamed soft and reptilian in the sunlight.

The well-oiled lid opened silently and exposed tantalizing glimpses of the contents within.

Butch hefted each piece and weighed them gently in his hands before deciding which would be used first.

Ah, yes. There it was- glowing in the depths of the box.

Tenderly, Butch reached in and curled his fingers around one of his favorites- Estwing's German Pattern Latthammer; solid polished magnified steel with a beautiful patterned leather grip, the head and handle forged in one piece- a mere 13 inches long, but what a powerhouse.

Pausing to admire the head, he tilted it this way and that, and suddenly he saw her- reflected in the cool steel as though delicately daubed there by god's own paintbrush.

But it wasn't a painting. He took in the sparkling yet sultry eyes, a captivating and alluring smile haloed by the most glorious hair he'd ever seen.

He knew right then his life would never be the same.

Chapter Two- Thrill of the Chase

The Range was a safe zone, and not everyone knew where it was. Therefore, everyone knew everyone else there...most of the time.

Butch lowered the Estwing, and turned around slowly- holding his breath as though afraid she'd be gone...just a figment of his imagination.

And yet, there she was- even more beautiful than her reflection. Butch cleared his throat, raised one eyebrow nonchalantly while his eyes played over her from top to bottom and back again...slowly and appreciatively.

Her hair wasn't so much a color as an aurora of copper and bronze and gold; it moved on its own in undulating waves of sensuality. Brown eyes flecked with green nestled on either side of a seriously straight yet dainty nose and over full soft lips that were devoid of artificial color or moisture, yet pulsed with sexuality. Butch wanted those lips- wanted to feel them slowly exploring every inch of his body and his jeans were suddenly too tight for him.

She was outstandingly fit and muscular, yet soft and supple and just a few inches shorter than he was. Her kid leather vest laced just to the top of her lace camisole. Breasts rising and falling with her slow steady breathing showed only a dew of perspiration; just enough to intensify and carry her scent of leather, and sunshine, and Black Orchid to him where it wafted up into his sinuses and took root in his brain- where he'd never forget it.

Her jeans were cut low and there was just an inch of perfect flesh between the bottom of the vest and the top of the faded and form-fitting Levi's.

Her feet were bare; her toenails polished blood red in direct contrast to her fingernails, which were as unadorned as her lips- on her ring finger of her right hand was a band of silver set with a single moonstone. She wore no other jewelry.

He was accustomed to being met with blushing breathlessness or offended surprise after his predatory inventories, and was taken slightly aback to lift his eyes and meet her unwavering and slightly amused gaze.

Their eyes locked for one earth-shattering second and then she was gone.

Butch couldn't believe it.

One second she had been there- everything he'd ever wanted in every lust-filled dream he'd ever had…and then Little Bobby had lumbered in between them with his tool in one hand and a newly cracked Coors in the other and she'd vanished into thin air.

Little Bobby was about 6'8" tall and weighed in at well-nigh 300 pounds. His dad, Big Bobby (all 5'7" and 130 pounds of him) referred to the fruit of his loins as 'useless as tits on a boar hog', but most everyone tolerated his vulgar shenanigans because he was, after all, one of their own…and they were all a little afraid of him, though they'd never admit to it.

Little Bobby was known to be 'a tad rough' with the ladies, so in true deep-woods Southern fashion, all the ladies were warned to keep an eye out and stay far clear of him.

Because Boys will be Boys.

When little five-foot-nuthin' and light as a feather AmyJo Williams ended up in the hospital with severe blunt trauma injuries in places that were obvious, and some that weren't talked about by good church-going folks it was the un-official talk of the town. With her golden hair peeking out from her bandages and the tears squeezing painfully out of blackened eyes, she whispered to the deputies that it had been Little Bobby who'd done it.

"I got off my shift at the Sonic at 10pm and he was waiting in the backseat of my car. I told him I'm only 15 and don't even have a boyfriend and he laughed and said 'You do, now, darlin'. My daddy always told me to steer clear of Bobby, but I thought it was just because he's a little strange. He never told me I had to be afraid of him. Now I'm afraid all the time. I don't even want to close my eyes at night, even here in the hospital. I'll never feel safe again. Doc said there was a lot of tearing and I may not be able to have any kids now. Don't matter much- I'm never letting anyone near me, no how".

Community reaction was predictable. Little Bobby was summarily hauled in and questioned. His buddies Skeeter and Pud both swore on the bible that Bobby had been with them shinin' deer that night…and Bobby was a free man who owed Skeeter and Pud big-time. In their circle you always got your friends' backs and 'big-time' meant a few cases of Coors.

The women knew there was nothing they could do- they'd been taught their entire lives that men were the masters of the earth and women their helpmeets. Underneath their stoic exteriors they every last one of them wanted to castrate Little Bobby with their bare hands and beat him to death with his own penis.

Then they prayed for grace and mercy and redoubled their warnings to their daughter, their mothers and each other to 'steer clear of Little Bobby'.

Then they tried to convince themselves that somehow, somewhy it was really AmyJo's fault; she should've never agreed to work the late shift (even though her family desperately needed the money and she was in high school the rest of the day), she should've never worn that provocative outfit (her SONIC uniform? Well...we *were* talking about Little Bobby, here).

Because otherwise what happened to AmyJo could happen to their daughters, their mothers, themselves. So they pent it all up and tied it off neatly with the Scriptures and locked it away in an inaccessible corner of their minds.

What looked like devoted obedience to their place in the world from the outside was barely-contained rage and frustration, and they listened to their preachers and their husbands and tried to believe that it was because they were fallen and lesser and took that to their hearts and tried to do better, to be better, to be impossible.

Butch had spent his whole life with this type of woman. Like most of the people in these parts, he'd never really been anywhere except for his four years in the service, which gave him authority to say he'd 'seen the world'.

Seeing the world in the military is like thinking plants only grow above ground. There is a real and necessary divide between a 'visiting' military presence and the local populace; necessary because at any given moment, the command may come down to stop keeping the peace and start shooting people, and nothing will cause a pause in a trigger finger more than aiming your weapon at a target you've had dinner with, drunk a beer with, know the children and grandparents of.

So for the most part, the military version of 'seeing the world' is highly select and not much good except to form the most general of opinions; "Those are a very clean people", "They are very hard workers", "Most immaculate whore house I've ever been to".

So Butch's experience with women could be categorized as 'narrow yet active'- there were always the 'bad girls' in town, the easy ones who went to church every Wednesday and Sunday and the pool hall every Friday and Saturday. How they squared what they heard from their parents and the pulpit with what they did with every fella in town he never could quite figure out, but that wasn't his problem.

It was his pleasure.

The bad girls were fun and the good girls were fundamentals and there was a time and a place for both types. The good girls you took out in public and eventually married. The bad girls you took to bed even after you married a good girl…because good girls have a tendency to not quite give in completely to the lush variety of carnal pleasures.

It's all well and good to make love with your prim and proper wife who's never had sex with anyone else. I mean, all sex is good sex, right?

There's just something about a woman who's had multiple lovers and who doesn't give a rat's ass about what society says she 'should' be doing or not. Something more fun, more…sexy, dammit.

So he tolerated the good girls, enjoyed the hell out of the whores and appreciated the skills of the prostitutes at every port of call, but the woman reflected in the glow of the latthammer had been a different creature altogether.

"Dammit, Little Bobby!" Butch pushed the clueless Bobby out of the way to no avail.

Looking around almost frantically, he asked everyone and no one in particular if they'd seen her, knew who she was and where she had come from and gone to.

Someone had to know, since the security was pretty tight at the Range.

In order to get in, you had to know someone already a member or pass a pretty strict background check. Because you just couldn't be too careful these days.

It didn't used to be this way.

Used to be you could open carry anything you liked anywhere you wanted to. No one cared and everyone respected a man (or woman) and their freedom to be responsible for their own security.

Then the trouble started.

That goddamn NRA.

They'd always been unlikable pricks; going on and on about the 2nd Amendment and hollering that it there were no limits to it, when any fool could see that just like there's a reason rocket-fueled race cars are not street legal, common sense dictates that free, easy and unlimited access to something that's sole purpose is to put a hole in a living thing and make it dead is a recipe for disaster.

Any fool could see right through the propaganda and marketing the NRA used- paid for by the gun manufacturers and lapped up by the misguided; who created every shortage of guns and ammo the industry screamed to watch out for.

All you had to do was listen to their drivel for a few minutes about "The Sanctity of the Armed Citizen" and then say something like, "That's an excellent idea- people DO need to feel safe- when are you going to arm all the poor people in the ghettos?" to see their 'Great Equalizer' hoo-ha fall apart at the seams.

As society fell into economic disarray, it became obvious to most folks that easy access to any and all firearms were making us much less safe instead of safer. As more and more people's sanity stretched and then snapped, more and more innocents were killed by 'responsible gun owners' in 'unfortunate but unavoidable accidents'.

The populace began to insist on some common sense regulations.

The gun lobby countered that that was a Slippery Slope to total government disarmament and trotted out the spectre of Nazi Germany- hoping no one would notice the complete lack of correlation between pre-Nazi Germany and the USA, and *really* hoping that no one would notice how much safer all those other civilized countries were with much stricter gun laws.

Sad to say- people actually did notice those things, and it was painfully apparent that the Day of the Gun was over in the US of A.

Unless.

Unless they could find and hold up something even *more* dangerous, more common and more violent than a firearm for the citizens to demonize and the lawmakers to outlaw.

So they did. And now Butch and everyone like him suffered, as well as the rest of society.

God damn NRA.

Sighing with frustration, Butch reached back into the tool box and was fingers' touch from the still-waiting Estwing when he felt warm breath on his neck gently blowing leather and sunshine and Black Orchid straight through his skin, and he froze.

"I'm right here, Bubba" came the low, slow whisper followed by a throaty chuckle.

Quick as a snake bite Butch spun around and found himself touching her from nose to toes. Imperceptibly and unconsciously they leaned into each other; foreheads, noses, chins, torsos, pelvises, knees and toes matched up in a mirror of desire.

"Have you been looking for me as long as I've been looking for you?" His words got tangled in the wild mane of hair they were spoken into, and for the first time in his life that tired old pick-up line rang true.

"I believe just a bit longer than that", she whispered directly into his ear; goose bumps ran up his arms like dominoes on crack.

They leaned impossibly closer together and their mouths met with the power of unbridled electricity; their lips opened slightly, questioningly, tongues barely touching and then...

...the sound of fireworks, just like in the movies.

But it wasn't fireworks at all- it was gunfire.

The Range was being raided.

Chapter Three- Foreplay

Butch's brain registered several things at once- the woman was no longer in front of him but had swooped up most of the items in his toolbox with one hand, grabbed his hand in the other and was dragging him expertly through the maze of confusion and into the woods that ringed the Range.

People around them were running, screaming, dropping to the ground from fear or gunfire yet the glorious head of hair in front of him never slowed down or wavered in the face of gunshots or the deep underbrush of the forest.

He thought with alarm about his truck being left behind, with concern for his friends still at the Range, and with total amazement that that she could run so quickly barefoot over the rocks and branches, thorned vines and hot sand.

After what seemed like the better part of a mile, she yanked him around to the far side of an enormous tree and they leaned up against it for a few minutes, gasping in unison.

Finally, Butch looked at her quizzically and asked, "Who *are* you and where did you come from?"

Brown eyes sparkled at him. "I'm your Guardian Angel, Bubba. And we're going home".

She turned on her heel and started off again, not seeming to care if he followed or not.

Butch shrugged and tagged along- this day couldn't possibly get any more strange.

"You know, I could take a few of those if you like…since they're mine and all. Unless you like toting around over fifty pounds of dead weight" he suggested.

She stopped in mid-step and turned around, her hair ethereally backlit by the lowering sun. "Don't be silly, Bubba- you weigh much more than fifty pounds and I don't mind at all".

His tongue tied his feet to the ground for just a few seconds and his eyebrow came up. No woman had ever talked to him like that before.

He was almost certain he wasn't supposed to approve of it.

Almost.

She was nearly out of sight, so he trotted to catch up. They rounded the base of a steep bluff and he knew the day was, in fact, getting stranger by the minute.

The small compound was alive with activity. Everyone was building something. From furniture to picture frames the entire area was filled with creation of some sort and the air echoed with the sound of hammering.

Beautiful hammering.

Wonderful hammering.

Illegal as hell hammering.

When the NRA had cleverly deflected public opinion by publishing study after study and article after article and had purchased enough politicians to make a legislative difference, it had spelled the end of freedom for Butch and every American like him- carpenters.

The NRA gleefully punted the ball to the far-right GOP, fundamental Southern Christians, the Tea Party and FOX News and they ran with it, baby.

It was everywhere on the TV and the internet with graphic photographs of horrific injuries and interviews with families in shock that they themselves had been affected by something that was so common and seemingly safe.

"FBI figures prove- more people in America killed by hammers than by guns!"

"Gun violence? What about hammer violence? America's Secret Shame!"

"Hammers WAY more dangerous than guns! Why are they not regulated???"

And finally, the death blow-

"NRA demands and spearheads hammer-control legislation to save innocent Americans from senseless violence! God Bless the NRA!"

Oh, sure the builders' unions had tried to fight it. The corporate giants like Home Depot and Lowe's had thrown tons of money into the huge legal-defense pot. Average American do-it-yourselfers had picketed and marched and written their congressmen by the hundreds of thousands... but to no avail.

When the contractors asked how they were supposed to build houses and whatnot now, they were told, "Screw it!" and studies were produced (paid for by the NRA) showing that things that are screwed together are actually stronger than those that are nailed.

And so it went.

Hammers were outlawed and now only outlaws had hammers.

Anyone who wanted to still build anything with nails had to do so in private and in hiding- in places like the Range; where small groups of people gathered for an afternoon and then disbursed, leaving no trace of their activity.

Where they were now was something completely different.

This was bigger, and permanent, and damn impressive.

"OK, pretty lady- explain this to me," Butch demanded after taking it all in for a few minutes.

She smiled slowly and winked at him. "Geez, Bubba- you never heard of a BRAD before?"

Of course he had, but he'd never known of one in practice- certainly not this close to home. He and everyone he knew assumed if there were any BRAD's in existence, they were all in remote mountain hideaways, not just a few miles outside of a town of 100,000.

BRAD was an acronym for Builders Reconstructing the American Dream, using the term for a small yet sturdy type of nail, and they were literally guerilla warriors in the war on traditional construction.

Furtively, they moved in society- quietly observing the sometimes slow, sometime sudden deterioration of infrastructure without the benefit of hammer and nails.

Secretly, they offered their services to people they had ascertained were a safe risk.

If it was a small job, they'd take it back to the BRAD to work on, but if it was a large job, they'd work undercover of thundery windy nights to muffle the sound of their labor- real life storm troopers.

It was dangerous and intense work and they recruited every expert they possibly could...which is why Butch had been singled out to join them.

The initial plan had been to merely pitch the idea to him, but Fate had literally pitched him headfirst into it without benefit of thinking about it first.

"Your name is Fate?" he asked with a frown later in the privacy of her little home in the compound. It was late and there was only the one bed. They lay next to each other in the dark and talked casually while thinking sensuously.

"What kind of mother names her daughter 'Fate'?"

She laughed at him and explained that her parents had tried for years to get pregnant with no luck. When her father was diagnosed with advanced cancer, they put parenthood on the back burner...until the 3rd missed period when her mother had finally noticed the change in herself and went to the doctor for confirmation.

Long-awaited daughter of Tom and Janet Devine, Fate had been born just a month before her father died.

Butch nodded. "And what does your mother think of her daughter running barefoot through the woods with strange men?"

A shadow crossed her beautiful face. "Not much- she died a few years ago. Shot accidentally while on her own front porch by a neighbor figuring out his new gun under the expert guidance of his buddies and a few beers".

"Jesus, I'm so sorry. And yet it's hammers they outlawed. What kind of crazy country are we living in?" Butch slid closer and put his arms around her protectively.

Almost violently she pulled away. "It's not the guns, or the hammers- they're both inanimate objects. It's our pathetic worship or irrational fear of things that are mere tools making us crazy- making us fight for our 'freedom' to own or restrict the tools more than to protect the lives they may impact".

They fell asleep back to back in stony uncomfortable silence.

Butch roused just a bit to the aroma of Black Orchid and the light touch of his shirt buttons being undone.

Soft kisses, no more than angel pecks, started on his forehead, his closed eyelids, his cheeks. Ever so fleetingly, his lips were brushed and then his face was buried in a cloud of long hair as lips and tongue explored his neck, his chest, and down to his abdomen; kissing, tasting, nibbling.

He could swear what was happening was real, yet he couldn't seem to move or open his eyes so his brain logically assumed he was dreaming. There was no other explanation since if it were really occurring he'd be wide awake and reciprocating.

No doubt about it.

Fate's hot breath moved lower still and he tried to arch his back and hips upward to meet her mouth but he remained inexplicably locked in place.

Slowly at first, then quicker and more urgently she kissed, fondled, stroked his erect manhood until he climaxed...still he was unable to move anything but what she brought to life and fruition.

He woke as the sun rose and they were still back to back and fully dressed. Slipping out of the bed as quietly as possible to head for the bathroom, he glanced at Fate.

She was sound asleep.

And smiling.

Chapter Four- Stimulation

She never said a word at breakfast that didn't have to do with explaining the BRAD to him- who was there, where they came from and how they accomplished what they did. He understood the 'why' of it all.

You just couldn't build anything properly without nails, and without hammers nails were useless. It was ridiculous to expect carpenters to work without hammers; ridiculous to label all hammers as dangerous when they ranged from the tee-tiniest 3-ounce brass jewelry mallets to the frightening and aggressive M48 Kommando Tactical Survival Hammers and everything in between.

But none had been spared. The reasoning was that no exceptions could be made, no tolerance given.

The whole 'slippery slope' argument had been trotted out and paddled around till those in charge were sure it was god's own truth and the skeptics were drowned out in its wake.

And so it went. No hammers allowed. Certain tradesmen were cleared to own certain hammers as long as they were registered and licensed, and the owners had completed government-sponsored and written safety courses, which all had to be renewed every year. But the average layman?

No way, no how, no hammers.

The once-great nation that had been built literally to the music of hammer and nails quickly fell into disarray and disrepair and the citizens were told, "It's all worth it to ensure the safety of everyone...especially the children. You *do* want your children to be safe, don't you?"

Of course they did.

But the children weren't any safer at all.

Accidental shootings accelerated, domestic violence by firearm skyrocketed, mass murders continued unabated and it was all downplayed in the news.

Because everyone knew where the real danger was.

Hammers.

And the goddamn NRA smiled and sat back and counted their money. Their glorious, blood-soaked money.

So it was up to the rebels in the shadows to keep America strong and in good repair. And that was the 'why' in a nutshell.

'Who' was the best of the contractors and tradesmen. BRAD sponsors kept watch and solicited and asked around surreptitiously to find carpenters of exceptional skill. They used recruiters like Fate to make the offer appealing and irresistible.

Butch couldn't take his eyes off of her. She was appealing and irresistible.

Finally he couldn't stand it anymore.

"Goddamn, girl- tell me what you did to me last night! Not that I didn't enjoy it- don't get me wrong, but how did you do it?" Butch winked at her boyishly, trying to cover the strange blend of uneasiness and desire welling up inside of him.

Fate stopped mid-bite and cocked her head to one side; a devious gorgeous little bird. "I have no idea what you're talking about", she said matter-of-factly, and turned her attention to the last swallow of coffee in her mug. Over the rim of the ceramic, her eyes flashed at him teasingly, and then closed.

If there were such a thing as a double wink, he'd just witnessed it.

Chapter Five- Penetration

It was cloudy and calm, with the foreboding quiet that comes before a storm and the inhabitants of the BRAD knew they'd have time later in the day to work on their current project; the local school needed many interior repairs that were not getting done with the shortage of carpenters who were licensed to carry.

The secret was getting in before the school was locked up for the day, and getting out before anyone showed up the next morning. Only one person was allowed to 'officially' know about the BRAD- the janitor who would work side by side with them all night, and then mop up spilled goulash and tempera paint all the next day.

Of course all the teachers and students knew what was going on- how else to explain desks that were repaired, locker doors that hung correctly, windows that slid open and shut with one finger instead of two fists.

But they looked the other way and didn't say anything out loud, just sent their thanks along with the janitor, who passed it down the line.

Fate and Butch worked side by side getting tools together and in order, and he couldn't help but notice every detail of her while they were in such close proximity.

She had a way of pursing her lips in concentration that was both darling and erotic, her hands were soft but tough and her blue jeans showed off every womanly curve.

It was warm in the tool shed, and her breasts shimmered with perspiration- the heat amplifying the scent of her, making him almost crazy.

Fate was doing her best to be casually businesslike, but it took everything she had.

Outwardly, she arranged and handed him what they'd need for their evening's work but inwardly she relived last night vividly in her head.

Every sense had been alive, twice alive since he'd been unable to move and she'd experienced both of their sensations.

She knew she shouldn't have done it. Nothing would be gained by becoming involved, and so much could be lost.

They were too different- brought together by circumstance, yes. But it was impossible to think they could stay together.

There was just something about him.

Despite her careful guarded training, last night came flooding back into her thoughts: his breath shallow and expectant as she undressed him, the taste of him-all of him everywhere, the feel of his taut body straining up towards her, and the sound and scent of his coming all vividly etched in her mind.

She'd done it many times before with many different lovers; casting the spell that paralyzed them was her way of keeping them literally at arm's length where they couldn't get too close, couldn't hurt her physically or emotionally.

Or so she had thought till last night.

There was just something about him.

Fate was relieved that they'd be busy today and tonight, relieved that by the time they got home they'd be dead tired…or at least she could pretend to be.

Because she was just not going there.

Life is difficult when you're different from the other kids.

Growing up without a dad was tough. Growing up without siblings was tougher. Growing up with powers was almost unbearable. Her mother comforted her and trained her to control herself as well as her surroundings and those close to her- all with kindness and gentleness, never out of anger or spite.

When her mother was killed, Fate almost went completely mad. She was totally alone in a world that didn't make any sense and was falling apart at the seams.

She didn't fit in anywhere but felt a strangely maternal protectiveness for almost everyone, because in this new world everyone was trying desperately to figure out where they now fit in.

When she'd heard about the BRAD, she knew she needed to help out as much as she could. So she went down into the basement of their house where her dad had had his workshop. Her mother had closed the door on it the day he died and storage boxes had been piled in front of it.

Taking a deep breath, Fate pushed all the boxes out of the way and opened the door, sneezing at the dust whirling around her head.

She felt the sadness twirling in the dust motes and knew her mother's presence was in the room with her. She suddenly was overcome with how very alone she was and she sank to the floor, resting her head on the big metal tool box.

Sniffles turned to tears turned to sobs as the sun lowered silently beneath the horizon.

"Oh, mom. I don't know what to do. I don't know how to help. I just don't know anything anymore".

"Open the box, baby. Just open the box."

And there they were.

Her dad's hammers glowed silver and solid underneath his favorite photographs.

Her mother and father on their wedding day.

Her mother holding a tiny newborn Fate.

And one of her mother that she'd never seen before. Filled with shadows and blurred with under-exposure, the full moon was the only illumination, rendering the image shades of black and white even though it had been taken with color film.

It was of the woods behind their house- the same woods that the bullet that had killed her had careened through, and the soft image seemed ethereal and visceral in its feminine power, naked save the gossamer cloak, bare feet not touching the ground, her mother's hair flowed behind her- golden waves in a velvet night.

Fate couldn't stop staring at it, couldn't feel herself breathing as she felt her mother there in the photo, there beside her; and she knew her mother would never really leave her.

She felt her mother's love and sadness, futile despair at the cancer she couldn't stop and the death she couldn't change, the loss of her life's love almost unbearable. If she hadn't had Fate to raise and care for, there was no doubt she would've taken her own life to avoid the pain of it.

But she'd done what needed doing, and now here was her daughter all grown up- as beautiful and powerful as she had been.

"You have the power, the heart and the soul to do so much good, my daughter- don't ever forget that the power of good will always overcome evil, as

47

long as there is courage and sacrifice and more than a little bravado."

Fate smiled through her tears, tucked the photographs into her pocket, picked up her father's tool box and walked out of the house for the last time.

It was her dad's toolbox they were stocking right now, and Butch's hand brushed hers for just an instant.

He couldn't figure her out.

What had happened last night flummoxed and puzzled him, but for some reason didn't frighten him, which was the most puzzling thing of all.

Butch had spent his whole life being the dominant one in any relationship, yet being rendered completely helpless had been the most erotic thing that had ever happened to him.

The tool box closed with a solid 'snap' and they looked at each other calmly, both of them hiding the emotions churning inside.

Side by side, Butch and Fate headed for the truck and the evening's work.

48

But both of them were thinking of what would, or would not, happen when they got back.

Chapter Sex

Fate sighed with exhaustion and turned off the light.

They were facing away from each other and their backs were almost but not quite touching. They were acutely aware of the closeness of the other's proximity.

Butch's eyes were closed and he tried to ignore the heat of her so close to him yet so far away. He had no idea what sort of mess he'd gotten himself into but he knew it was too late to get out. He was crazy about her, but a little voice inside him warned that she was just fucking crazy. He didn't care.

Fate's eyes were closed and she tried to ignore the heat of him so close to her yet so far away. She knew she had to be so very careful not to get involved- that proceeding any farther with this man would lead to nothing but heartbreak for them both, but she knew it was too late to get out. She was crazy about him- fucking crazy and she didn't care.

As if on cue they both inched almost imperceptibly closer to the other and their backs made contact from shoulder blades to buttocks. Ankles intertwining gently, the balls of their feet stroked against each other- the only motion on the bed.

Their breaths slowed and deepened, and without thinking about it or meaning to, they started breathing in rhythm.

A casual observer would think that there was only one organism on the bed from their synchronized outward movements, but inside their heads was a different story altogether.

Butch had always been a simple man. Not stupid or lazy, just 'simple' in the best possible definition of the word. He knew good from bad, right from wrong, up from down. He was good at being a carpenter, good with his hammers, good with his hands.

He was good with the ladies and he believed with all his heart that he was good *for* the ladies as well. He was polite and chivalrous, and made sure that any gal with him was safe and cared for. And all the other gals he'd been with appreciated the hell out of that.

He led and protected, they followed and were safe. Simple.

And now, this. This…whatever he'd gotten himself into with this woman who didn't fit into any mold in his experience. She made him feel like he was the most important man in the world while proving she didn't need him in the least. He had no earthly idea how to proceed with that. Every time he turned around Fate was leading the dance; shit- the night before he hadn't even been allowed to dance at all.

And what was up with that? Nothing in his past even came close to lining up with that, and yet he wasn't afraid or puzzled; he didn't care if he ever found out how she'd pulled that little stunt, because the very important thing- the *most* important thing was that right this minute he *was* able to move freely and touch her and there wasn't a single thing on earth he wanted more.

It was that simple.

"Stop. Stop now. Stop right now or something terrible is going to happen. You know there is no way this will turn out well." The voices In Fate's head were all in unison for once. Her instincts, her training, her emotions, the spirit of her mother all combined to beg her to stop this now- it wasn't in the agreement or the cards or the stars. Her life and his were meant to meet and travel side by side for a brief instant; not intermingle in any way.

She knew that in her head and her heart and down to her very toes…that were now working their way up and down his muscular calves.

She told her toes to stop that, but they kept at it defiantly.

Why did it have to be all so difficult? Why couldn't she just be an ordinary woman who wanted ordinary things; who was only capable of ordinary things and was content with that?

She'd been born different, of course. As had her mother and her grandmother and all the way back as far as recorded history reached, and then spiraling back even farther.

Even as a tiny child, she knew she was different from other children. She just felt things more acutely; not the everyday drama that comes with being small- all that stuff she brushed off without a second thought.

It was the big things that bothered her.

Why did the neighbor not pay any attention to the dog in his yard? She could feel the confusion and sadness emanating off of the big goofy hound dog as day after day his owner walked past him without even acknowledging the gift of devotion given freely with no resentment at affection unreturned.

How could that lady in the store yell at her child for something the child had no control over? Didn't she understand that the minor infraction in obedience would be forgotten within minutes but that her sharp words had already cut her child's fragile ego?

Things that most people didn't even see or feel, and if they did they ignored as 'unimportant and none of their business anyway'.

From a very early age, Fate took all that pain upon her tiny shoulders and into her heart- these things *were* important and they *were* her business- as a member of the human family it was all her business.

As she grew older and the world around her grew more fractured and wounded, her mother encouraged her to use her gifts to lessen the burdens and pains of her fellow humans, but warned her to always protect her very core from the worst of the emotional daggers.

As her toes traced Butch's calves she felt the loneliness jump from him to her and run up her legs and into her gut.

Mr. Man About Town, who exuded only confidence wrapped in bravado bathed in testosterone to the entire world, had had many partners but no lovers.

She knew absolutely that what she was about to do was wrong- not 'wrong' in the moral sense since morality is merely subjective, but 'wrong' in the grand scheme of things…wrong for her and wrong for him.

But damn it- he was just so needy. Needy and something else she couldn't quite put her finger on.

And so very sexy.

Without thinking, she had turned over and was now nuzzling the small of his back, and her fingers played along his arms softly. She inhaled the good clean scent of him, regretting in advance what they were about to do…what *she* was about to do with no spell between them keeping them both safe. Right this minute he was able to move freely and touch her and there wasn't a single thing on earth she wanted more.

It was that simple.

Chapter Seven- Climax

Slowly, as if afraid any sudden movement would cause him to be rendered immobile again, Butch turned to meet her.

He could still move.

Their eyes met and locked for what seemed an eternity, and he reached out to touch her face tenderly.

"You know I won't hurt you, right?" he whispered. "No matter what happens tonight- I'll never hurt you".

"I'm not afraid of you hurting me, darlin'. I'm a lot tougher than I look", she tried to lighten the moment and push the warning bells to the back of her brain so she could concentrate on the immense and electrical contentment she felt with her entire body touching his entire body; nose to toes.

Of course Fate was already familiar with every inch of Butch's body, but this was deliciously different because the sensations were now shared and reciprocated, matched touch for touch, tongue for tongue.

They kissed, tenderly at first and then deeper and more insistent, their fingers petting and stroking and seeking; needing to know each other every inch and knowing that what they needed was right there within reach, within touch.

Side by side, face to face, Butch pulled his face back just a bit and whispered, "Now?"

Fate nodded and sighed and wrapped her leg over and around him, curling her pelvis in to meet his hips.

They kissed again, tongues flickering in and out and their arms held tight to each other- fingers gently raking each other's back as he entered her smoothly and began the age-old rhythm of mating on this blue green speck hurtling through the blackness of the universe.

Tiny as dust motes, insignificant as grains of sand, this absolutely natural and ordinary coming together of two beings never fails to be astounding in its power, breathtaking in its complete abandonment of self to mere instinct.

They ceased kissing and her head tucked under his chin and up against his neck, her breath warm and moist on his skin. He breathed in the fragrance of her hair, felt her breasts against his chest and her leg clutching him tight to her, holding him inside of her till they both shuddered and relaxed.

Their heartbeats echoed in their ears, staccato like hammers, like gunfire.

Gunfire.

Fate clutched the covers around herself and peered out of the window, the voices in her head moaning in despair.

Next to her in the bed she heard Butch whisper under his breath, "Shit".

Slowly she turned to him and asked as coolly and calmly as she could, "Butch? What's going on?"

She felt the sticky sweetness of him puddling beneath her, warm as blood.

"Butch?"

"They weren't supposed to come when anyone was here", he whispered in the dark.

Outside, the night started to glow orange and yellow with flames.

"What are you talking about? Who is out there and what are they doing?"

He started to explain, started to make excuses, but she didn't have time. There was no time.

Fate grabbed his face in her hands and looked deep into his eyes, seeing what he'd done to the BRAD and all the people in it, what he'd done to her.

He'd been gone only a few minutes while they were working at the school- she figured he'd needed to pee and hadn't thought twice about it. Now she realized he'd been contacting the authorities to tell them where they were hiding.

The guns had stopped firing and the night blazed brighter, the sound of muffled explosions replacing the sharp reports of bullets. Everything was on fire, crumbling.

She could hear, could *feel* people trapped and suffering. She was dressed and at the door in a matter of seconds and he reached out desperately and latched onto her wrist.

"I'm so sorry- no one was supposed to be here when they came. They promised me no one would be here when they came- you have to believe me!"

"I'm sorry too, Bubba and of course I believe you- you're a good man at heart and you'd never hurt anyone on purpose." Her face was impassive and unreadable, betraying the raw sorrow she felt as she ruffled his hair maternally.

59

"I understand you want to check on everyone- be sure everyone's OK. I'll be right here when you get back and we'll talk about it". Fate wasn't sure if she should spit on him or slap him so she did neither.

"Sure, Butch- you can tell me all about it later". She turned away from him and walked out the door.

When the building exploded she didn't even slow down or turn her head.

<u>Epilogue</u>

Butch's head slowly shook side to side in disbelief. His eyes stared straight ahead in surprise.

Of course it was just the momentum of the moment and the fact of being rounded that his head moved at all.

Lodged neatly and on edge betwixt his head and the rest of him was most of the plate glass window from the ruined and twisted story above him. The incessant pounding from the sledgehammer had first loosened it from what was left of its frame and finally, with a final and fateful shudder of climax the glass released itself and gave in completely to gravity, not even pausing while passing through that eight inches of human flesh and bone that used to be Butch's neck.

The Wilton 20 was still, coated with the aftermath of its final explosive efforts. The air was filled with the musk of blood and dust and fire, leather and sunshine and Black Orchid.

Butch's fingers wrapped clawlike around the thirty six inch vulcanized rubber and tempered steel rod handle and they turned from lifelike pinkish tan to fish-flesh white in just a few minutes as his body quickly bled out in a silent puddling- first pulsing quick and hot from the almost surgical slice and then gradually slower and slower till it finally trembled to a standstill… but they never loosed their grip.

Muscle memory.

A warm breath of a breeze gently ruffled his full head of raven hair one last time, and a long drawn-out sigh filled with regret balanced in the air for a moment, then faded away on a wisp of Black Orchid.

BOOK TWO-

AN UNHEALTHY

OBSESSION

Prologue

Their laughter wafted through the smoke-filled room, causing her to involuntarily shudder. Anytime these guys laughed it meant that they were talking about the suffering of someone or something innocent.

They made her skin crawl, but she put on her hardened-barmaid face and approached the table in the corner. "You boys need another round?" she asked with a tired smile, putting her hand on JR's shoulder with familiarity- hoping her revulsion didn't show.

"Yeah, yeah- in a second, babe- first you gotta hear this! This is the funniest shit I've ever heard- tell her, Dickie! Tell her just like you told us!"

Sighing silently and mentally rolling her eyeballs, Fate turned just a bit to face Dickie and give the appearance of giving a damn.

Dickie puffed all up to his full 5'6" at being the center of attention for once and he squinted as he tried mightily to remember exactly how he had told it so it would come out just as perfectly this time as well. Sweat beaded on his forehead under his unkempt hair hidden under an ancient feed store cap that matched his overalls and torn dirty work shirt.

He smelt rather strongly of perspiration and beef jerky, cheap cigarettes and gallons of beer.

Finally, he opened his eyes and tried to focus roughly in the area of her straight perfect nose. Or maybe her lips; full and soft, yet free of lipstick. Possibly her cheekbones, high and elegant.

But definitely not her breasts. The one man who had stared too boldy and overlong there had encountered first her backhand across his face and then an unfortunate and sudden injury to his manly bits, dropping to the floor as though kicked by a bull, even though she hadn't moved anything but her hand.

Fate had immediately helped him up and mumbled, "Sorry- didn't mean to hit you that hard", but after that all the guys were very careful to stare anywhere but…there.

There were plenty of other nice parts to stare at. Her hair always managed to stay not quite contained up in the admittedly haphazard bun she wore in a hat-tip to the laughable "health code" not even enforced in a corner tavern that served food. Frothy tendrils in hues of precious metals softened her normally guarded expression.

She wore a single coat of mascara on her long lashes; a protective jet black barricade for her brown eyes flecked with green to nestle behind, but that was her only makeup. Her hands were strong and her nails short and clean; neither buffed nor polished.

Her stereotypical 'barmaid' outfit seemed designed for her body alone- the low-cut white cotton peasant blouse perfectly displaying cleavage that boys' fantasies start with, short and tight leather skirt accentuating her muscular and totally feminine buttocks, and the hated ridiculous fishnet stockings ensnared her impossibly long legs; impossible since she was barely over 5 feet tall all told.

She had needed the money badly, so she'd taken the job and the uniform, but had drawn the line firmly at footwear. There was no way she was going to wear 4 inch "knock me down/fuck me" heels on a job where she'd be on her feet for ten hours at a stretch. No way.

Eddie had glared at her. Most women backed down at 'the glare', but Fate had returned it unwaveringly, and he'd acquiesced. Her first day at work he had to acknowledge that far from detracting from the desired look, for some reason the sensible soft leather ballerina flats she had chosen to wear only made her look even more sexy.

And that, of course, was what he was looking for. Because he expected his girls to be 'full service with a smile'.

"DICKIE! Jesus! We don't have all night!" JR's caustic voice jolted Dickie back from his 'looking everywhere but Miss Fate's boobies' trance.

He cleared his throat, made a muffled gargling noise and spit onto the floor; a pre-show warm-up.

"Well, Miss Fate- I was just tellin' the boys here about the damnedest thing. I went out to do chores this morning for my momma and found her two ducks stone cold dead in the water trough. In the water!"

There was renewed chuckling as his audience imagined the scene.

"Yes, ma'am- those ducks had flat *drowned*! Now how the Sam Hell does a duck *drown*?"

Dickie looked puzzled and not at all amused- he actually seemed more disturbed by the incident than humored by it, but his comrades were unanimously cackling and hooting thinking about such a ridiculous thing- drowning ducks.

Fate closed her eyes and the images came to her.

Two half-grown ducks in a smallish water trough- not much bigger than a bucket, really. The water was not deep- they could've stood up in it easily. One tried to hop out and slipped, briefly going head-under upside-down.

The hapless duckling panicked, causing the other one to instantly be filled with fear as well.

Her mind's eye watched in hopeless horror as the ducklings pushed each other under the surface over and over again as they tried to clamor out of the water…and then they were still.

"That *is* weird, Dickie, but you know fear is a powerful force- I hope your mom isn't too upset losing her ducklings".

Dickie looked at Fate gratefully and said, "Well, she's pretty broke up about it, but I'm fixin' to get her some new ones next time I get a chance".

And Fate knew she'd be taking Dickie home with her at the end of her shift.

The others were still laughing and JR snorted and sneered, "What the hell? What do you expect of stupid ducks? Fucking bird-brains, right? Nothing to get all 'quacked up' about!" and everyone but Dickie and Fate grinned appreciatively at his masterful humor.

Chapter One- Dickie

Dickie watched Miss Fate make her way to the bar to fetch the next round. He'd worked his ass off all day hauling 50 pound sacks of feed and was exhausted and more than a little tipsy.

He'd been coming to Eddie's Place ever since it had opened the year he had turned 18 and he was pushing 40 now. Over twenty years, every single day after putting in his sixteen hours at the feed store hauling, toting, loading and unloading he came straight to Eddie's for just shy of an hour before heading home.

Home was where his momma was- widowed and alone except for Dickie. All the other kids had growed up and moved out and on- knocking the dust of this backwoods backwards town off their shoes the second they graduated high school.

Dickie had quit high school before sophomore year was out- that's the year his daddy had died and with Dickie being the oldest of the four kids, he was the one who had to get a job to help put food on the table.

His dad had worked as a mechanic at the Chevy dealership in town- had been there for over thirty years. When he had started there, he was a union member and the dealership had treated the workers fairly. Wages were good, and they had group health insurance- even a retirement 401k plan.

Then their state had become a 'right to work' state and the unions' backs were broken. All the big companies discontinued any benefits at all and as the economy grew worse, those employees who didn't get laid off or straight-up fired were given a big cut in pay.

Dickie's dad would come home dog-tired but resigned. "At least I still *have* a job- I'm one of the lucky ones!" he'd state, trying not to fall asleep in his dinner plate. When his cough turned into a hack, and the hack turned into a constant desperate wheeze, they scraped together enough money for a doctor exam. Because Dickie's mom was a nurse, they were able to wheedle imaging of the lungs out of the deal, but it really made no difference in the end result.

They buried Dickie's dad on a cold November afternoon- they had to work around his momma's schedule at the hospital since she wasn't allowed any time off for something as trivial as her husband of almost twenty year's funeral.

The cancer hadn't been that advanced when they first saw it.

Back when he'd had company insurance, they would've gone in and gotten it, zapped it with some chemo and the odds would've been very much in his favor to live a normal life to a normal old age. All this was accepted knowledge and procedure.

The problem was, of course, that without insurance, there was no money to do what needed done, and nowhere to turn to get any help except the loan sharks that had enjoyed a new resurgence, but Dickie's dad had refused to do that- he knew that if he went to the loan sharks and then died anyway, his family would lose everything.

This way they just lost him.

With the great 'Taking Back of America' that those on the far right had wrangled through concentrated fear-mongering, clever gerrymandering and copious bible-thumping had come the desired results. What the corporations that bought the politicians and elections didn't point out to their constituents was that the goal of 'Take Back America' was to take it *all the way* back to before unions, before social safety nets, before any regulations and restrictions that cramped the corporations' profit-based style.

So states adopted 'Right to Work' which decimated unions and should've really read 'Right to Work for Nothing', companies didn't have to provide any benefits *or* a living wage, and the ACA, which had been a tiny step towards the type of nationalized health care every other civilized nation on the planet had, had finally been recalled on the 60th attempt by Congress after the election of their Tea Party candidate as President. That president, along with the far right conservative Congress and Senate, had done what most people thought not only impossible but unthinkable- declared the Social Security and Disability programs as 'insolvent and unsustainable' and dismantled them with the promise of replacing them and the ACA with 'something better'.

And then they never did...just moved on and never looked back.

Anyone who had the audacity to question or complain was shamed into silence- didn't they *love* America? Didn't they *want* America to be strong and fiscally responsible again? Weren't they willing to make their small share of sacrifices for the future of *their children*?

Of course they were.

And so they died. By the thousands and tens of thousands they died. They died of things that could be cured easily with the right drugs and treatments- drugs and treatments that were now only available for those who had the cash to pay for them up front and outright.

They died for America and were buried with a folded flag under their head and a bible tucked under their hands.

They buried Dickie's dad with a folded flag under his head and a bible tucked under his hands and they turned away from the grave sick with loss and futility.

Dickie's mom had gone back to work the next day and Dickie had quit school the following week after securing employment at the feed store, and the younger kids did their time in school and were gone before the ink on their diplomas had dried because in their minds anywhere was better than this shithole of a town in this assbackwards southern state.

A few years later, Dickie's mom had wrenched the hell out of her back moving a patient and hurt herself worse than her doctor-employer could help her out with samples of painkillers and muscle relaxers passed under the table surreptitiously.

Without an MRI, there wasn't a back doctor anywhere who would see her- without proper imaging there was no way to know how to treat her, and there was no money for an MRI.

She worked till she just couldn't anymore, till she could barely get out of bed, till she couldn't sit upright without crying.

The day she quit work, she came home, put on her pajamas, crawled into bed with a coffee mug full of Sunset Blush (the finest of boxed wines) to dull the pain and waited to join her husband.

She didn't read. She didn't watch TV. When she did anything at all other than travel the path from the refrigerator with the wine box to the bathroom and back to the bed, she was looking out the window- it was the most mental stimulation she could handle through the pain and the fog of always being half tipsy.

Dickie doubled his hours at the feed store- took another guy's job when he quit after finding something not so mind-numbingly back-breaking, and no one cared. No one kept track of overtime anymore anyway.

He'd get up in the morning before daybreak to care for the little bit of livestock they had- enough chickens to keep them in eggs, a few rabbits for meat, and his mom's only pleasure- the ducks.

Something about ducks can make a stone gargoyle smile; some combination of ridiculous beak and webbed feet with a serious glare that defies any mocking under threat of bloody retribution. So even though the ducks didn't supply them with anything physically edible, they were a much-needed balm for her weary, sad and pain-filled soul.

Eyes following the antics of the ducks waddling along on their daily duck business, she'd smile ever so slightly, and shake her head just a bit to roll the unhappiness off to the side for just a moment and let this small pleasure take front and center for an instant.

When he found them dead, he was flabbergasted and horrified. He considered not telling his momma what had happened to them, but he could never lie to her- she'd see right through him.

She had tried to mask her feelings, but she'd never fully allowed herself to grieve for his dad, and now this outwardly little thing seemed to be the last straw.

"I see. Well, nothing to be done about it now". And she'd turned her head to the wall and stayed that way.

When he'd left for work, she hadn't moved.

Dickie finished up his beer and got up to go, passing by Fate on his way out the door. He stumbled just a bit with beer and fatigue and she put her hand out to steady him.

When he got into his truck, he looked down to put the key in the ignition and saw the piece of paper tucked into his pocket.

It was Fate's address and the notation, "One hour- take a shower" and a little winkie face.

Dickie stared at it owlishly, carefully folded it up the way it had been, tucked it back into his pocket and started the truck.

There were three stoplights between Eddie's Place and Dickie's house and he caught a red light at every single one. At every single one he'd take the note out of his pocket and read it again, then replace it folded as before.

When he pulled into his driveway he took it out one more time and really concentrated on it.

(Address) "One hour- take a shower" (wink)

Dickie shrugged and went inside to take a shower.

Momma was still facing the wall when he left, but she managed a muffled, "Be careful" to his, "I'm going out again for a bit- be home later, Momma".

Driving the short distance to Fate's place, Dickie didn't even try to make sense of it. He'd learned early that wonderful things just weren't going to happen to him; because of his circumstances and physical looks even the most normal of things people take for granted- finishing school, meeting someone, getting married, having kids- none of that was likely going to happen to him, and he'd come to terms with that.

But he also learned early on to never question chance, and to never look a gift horse in the mouth. This attitude had kept him mostly content. He was at ease with his lot in life, but never missed an opportunity for a brief glimpse of something more.

He'd never had a steady girl, but that didn't mean he'd never bedded a random one every so often. There are lonely people of both sexes, and sometimes ships don't just pass in the night, they collide for an hour, sometimes more, never an entire night, and even though the urge is strong and unstoppable, they sail on feeling emptier than before but somehow less alone.

If you looked up 'pragmatist' in the dictionary, you'd see a picture of Dickie. Not Dickie who had just left the tavern after a few beers and sixteen hours of physical labor, either. The cleaned-up version that was getting out of the truck now- freshly showered and hair slicked back...Formal Dickie.

Formal Dickie mustered up his courage, collected his nerves and knocked on the door, ready to stride back to his truck when no one answered.

Fate answered.

"Come in- and lock it behind you, please."

Dickie opened the door and was drawn in by the heady scent of Black Orchid- opulent, feminine, and overtly sexy without being overpowering.

"Miss Fate? It's me...Dickie". He locked the door behind him and made his way through the tiny but neat living room towards the door to the bedroom. He knocked on the door softly.

"I know it's you, Dickie- I put the note in your pocket". A throaty chuckle encouraged him to open the door.

She was on the bed, mostly naked. Her hair cascaded over her shoulders and her perfect cleavage peeked over the top of her lace camisole. Not that he looked there.

That was too dangerous.

Still a little too flummoxed to look her in her big brown eyes, terrified of looking anywhere in her 'breastal area', his gaze drifted further down and his mind registered while his groin verified that the camisole was, in fact, the only clothing she had on.

"Dickie? I won't bite you…unless you ask me real nice" and another soft chuckle.

Taking a deep breath, Dickie's eyes met hers. "Why? Why, Miss Fate?"

Fate looked at him, smiled, and answered as calmly and warmly as if they were fully dressed, standing in the grocery store produce aisle and were talking about the weather.

"Well, Dickie- because. Because you're a good man, and you have a good heart. You've worked damn hard all your life with damn little to show for it. You are honest and straightforward and take care of your momma when you could've just run off like the rest of your family- you were entitled to live your own life and you chose to do the right thing.

Because I find that very admirable and appealing and frankly very sexy. That's why."

Dickie thought about that for a minute. It all rang true and squared just fine in his head. He nodded more to himself than anyone else and started to get undressed.

As he carefully lifted the covers, he paused. "What about Eddie?"

"What *about* Eddie, Dickie?"she smiled.

"Well…aren't you supposed to, yanno, get paid for this and give him his cut?"

Fate sat up, looked him steadily and spoke firmly but kindly.

"Baby, I don't work for Eddie. Eddie and I have an understanding. He leaves me the fuck alone and I don't kill him". An angelic smile lit up her face and she gently kissed him on the lips.

Dickie's hands gently caressed her face, her neck and down to her breasts. Apparently, as long as you didn't *look* at them you were OK, because he was fondling them without any repercussion whatsoever.

He had heard rumors, of course, about Miss Fate Devine and her supposed 'powers', but there was nothing that he saw, felt or tasted that gave him pause or seemed in any way threatening, and she was just as gentle and soft with him as he was with her. When he finally rolled into position on top of her he paused just for a moment to etch the picture of her into his memory- from her hair fanning out on the pillowcase to her breasts (he plumb forgot not to look) and down her tanned and perfect tummy, to the amber-honey froth of hair between her impossibly long legs that were wrapped around his own, she was absolutely pure femininity.

She arched up to meet him and he was inside her and she around him, and they held each other for a long time in comfort and safety and a passion that was quiet yet intense, warmth without the pain of fire.

Fate had made them a cup of tea and they sat at her table companionably. He was dressed and she'd put a robe on. Her hair was, if possible, even more magnificent mussed up post-lovemaking.

"Thank you, Miss Fate. I had a right unforgettable time. I'm not a genius but I know this probably won't happen again, will it?" he smiled just a little sadly.

"No, Dickie, probably not. But you never can tell-stranger things have happened". And she kissed the top of his head and disappeared into the bathroom. He heard the sound of her in the shower.

Dickie waited a few minutes, unsure of what he was supposed to do now, and then cleared his throat, put the cups into the sink, rinsed them out and closed the door quietly behind him.

He walked just a little taller from her house to his truck and he knew if it had been anyone else, they'd drive straight to Eddie's and crow about it...telling every detail.

But that wasn't how he'd been raised and that wasn't what he would do. Private things stay private. They're sweeter that way, anyhow.

He was smiling as he got into the truck and he jumped just a little at the sounds coming from a cardboard box on the passenger seat. There was a soft scratching noise and an undeniable peeping.

"What the?" his brows furrowed. He'd locked the truck before going into her house- he always locked the truck.

Lifting the lid of the box, four little eyes stared back at him.

He'd kept ducks all his life, but he'd never seen any before that had brown eyes flecked with green.

<u>Eddie</u>

Over the rim of his raised glass, Eddie's eyes narrowed as he watched her slip the note into that idiot Dickie's shirt pocket.

If he didn't know better, he'd think that she was doing a little business of her own.

It made him crazy that she did what she wanted to, when she wanted to, with whom she wanted to and he couldn't do a damn thing about it. He was not accustomed to such autonomy in his girls, but since he'd hired this one, he'd had to get used to it.

His girls tended to come to him lacking. Lacking money, family, opportunity, options. Whether or not they lacked character and morals was not his concern and he didn't lose a minute of sleep over it- he provided a reasonably safe and secure income to women who were at the end of their ropes- he liked to think of himself as a bit of a kind-hearted philanthropist.

When Fate had showed up in his office looking for work, she didn't look any different than the others. Maybe a little less...used up looking, with a bit of a spark yet that hadn't been pissed on by Life, but basically she had been, you know...just another hard luck chick.

85

She'd answered all his questions in five words or less and he liked that- he didn't like to get all bogged down with the personal details of his girls. She'd taken the uniform he tossed at her without comment until he'd gotten to the shoes, and then she'd turned right obstinate. He told her that if she could prove to him she was just as sexy-lookin' wearing flats, she could keep 'em and he was astonished when she proved it beautifully but he couldn't go back on his word.

Because he prided himself on being a man of his word.

So the interview had gone well, and he ended it in his usual manner.

He'd bought her dinner at the local steakhouse and right between the main course and dessert he'd smiled sweetly and asked, "Your place or mine?"

"Excuse me?"

"Well, darlin'- Eddie don't sell nothin' he hasn't tried his own self...know what I mean?" and he winked in his best Favorite Lecherous Uncle manner.

"I'm sorry. I don't understand. I replied to the waitress ad- nothing else."

Eddie leaned forward, far enough for him to glance down into her very appealing cleavage, which he did, pointedly, and then said, "Oh, of course. You're a waitress. But if you recall, I did stress that keeping our customers happy was our number one priority- and at Eddie's Place, the waitresses are totally 'full service'…if you know what I mean". He winked again.

Leaning back into his chair, he smiled slowly and stated, "Unless you don't want the job after all. I understand and no hard feelings".

Fate didn't even hesitate. (None of them ever hesitated).

"My place. I'll be more comfortable there."

She motioned him to the sofa when they got to her little rent house. It was small but neat, sparsely furnished but cozy. "Could we have a cup of tea first? I just feel like I need to set a spell." Fate smiled at him, shyly.

Relaxing and stretching his legs out into the middle of the room, Eddie grinned generously and said, "Sure, Sugar- knock yerself out."

They drank their tea and he filled the silence with stories about all the girls who had worked for him and the girls still in his employ, and how much better their lives were now that they were turning tricks and making the big bucks for Saint Eddie. And he sounded sincere because he really believed it was true. He had single handedly improved the lives of many women one subsidized fuck at a time.

See, Eddie was a man of many virtues; that they all seemed to make him money was a happy side effect of the free market. He went on to tell her about his other social service.

Eddie's Place and its girls were small potatoes, actually. More of a recreational diversion. He made his real money in the health care field.

Oh, he wasn't a doctor or nurse. He was into the financing end of health care. People who needed expensive medical attention came to him and more often than not, he was able to 'work something out for them'.

Sure, the interest was high, somewhere in the neighborhood of 100%, and the penalties for non-payment were steep since Eddie insisted on holding vehicle and home titles as collateral, but times were hard, and when working with sick people you had to be careful to collect what you could when you could as quickly as you could, because if they ended up dead in spite of medical intervention, he hated how badly it reflected on his generosity when he seized people's transportation and kicked their families out of their homes.

It was just business, after all- nothing personal. And those people needed what he offered and had no other options…just like his girls.

Nowadays people like himself *were* the social safety net. God Bless America.

Their tea cups were empty and Eddie felt fine. He felt better than fine.

Fate was looking beautiful as the sun went down and the room dimmed naturally. She smiled sweetly and reached for his hand and led him into the bedroom.

He watched her undress and mentally patted himself on the back for hiring her- this one was absolutely top-shelf. He'd have to price her accordingly. Her price went even higher when she padded up to him on bare feet, no longer even a bit shy, and gently started unbuttoning his shirt.

He let her remove all his clothing and lead him to the bed. She placed a finger on his forehead, and softly traced a straight line slowly down his nose, over his lips, tickling and arousing every nerve in his neck, chest, abdomen and erect manhood.

And then they were on the bed together, kissing and touching, breathing and exploring.

They lay side by side facing each other, skin to skin from nose to toes. He gazed into her eyes- her brown eyes flecked with green. He was surrounded by the scent of Black Orchid and he smiled. Yes, she was definitely a high dollar fuck.

He kissed her as he entered her, slow and full.

Their tongues touched, stroked, circled each other smooth and warm…and just a little prickly and weird.

Just about then, he felt something…down under, and he pulled his head back just a bit in muddled and sex-concentrated confusion.

Focusing on her face, he saw her smile that sweet smile and her mouth opened just enough to let the huge hairy spider lazily crawl out of it and up her cheek; gently tapping her eyelashes before disappearing into her hair.

"Oh, shit!" Eddie jerked backwards away from her head but her arms and legs were locked around him and he was still inside of her, which was normally a good thing but something felt different, something was wrong.

He could feel himself moving but he wasn't thrusting, he was…swaying…sidewinding.

"Eddie dear- we need to have a little talk", Fate was being amiably, calmly sweet as honeysuckle in April.

"I am happy to be a waitress for you, I will wear that ridiculous demeaning costume for you, but I will never be 'one of your girls', you understand? Never. Not only that, but from this moment forward, you have no more 'girls'- you are absolutely out of the sex trafficking business. What your girls do or don't do is their business. We are all waitresses…period. Now, be a good boy and tell me you understand."

Eddie was frozen in place, his eyes trying to look into hers while darting back and forth on the lookout for that damn spider. "Yes. Yes- I understand! Sweet Jesus god almighty, I understand!"

"Good. Now put this thing back into your pants- I swear it's got a life of its own. I'm going to make some more tea- yaunt some?"

And she turned him loose and trotted back into the kitchen, naked and glorious, hair streaming behind her.

Perched on her left shoulder was the spider, and right before she disappeared from sight, he could swear he saw it pointing at the area below his belly button.

Eddie looked down slowly, his heart pounding out of his chest.

Looking back at him impassively was a flesh-colored snake with bright blue eyes attached to his body where his penis used to be.

He blinked and it blinked back. Its tongue darted out, tickling his belly button.

When he regained consciousness, he was in his own bed. Frantically he grabbed ahold of his crotch and was comforted by the wonderful familiar shape and fullness of his penis.

Of course it hadn't really happened. It must've been a hallucination- he must've gotten food poisoning or something and she'd taken him home and put him to bed. He'd been delirious or some such shit.

Damn that Mitchell at the steak house- Eddie had told him time and again not to buy the fucking discounted steaks from the refrigerator truck that parked in the liquor store parking lot.

Food poisoning. "Shit." Eddie whispered to himself.

He heaved an enormous sigh, and breathing in the scent of Black Orchid he looked down…and saw it.

In silent horror he gingerly peeled the snakeskin (complete with eye holes) off of his penis and on the black satin pillowcase next to his head was a message woven of spider silk-

"Remember our understanding, Sugar- I know you're a man of your word. Thank you for a wonderful time- Fate"

JR

JR watched Dickie weaving slightly on his way to the door and thought, "Poor bastard" to himself. JR and Dickie had gone to school together, grown up together, and were that curious blend of 'more than acquaintances but less than friends' that small towns produce out of people with very different personalities.

JR had never really understood what made Dickie tick. When they were in school, Dickie had always had an unnatural concern for other people- what they thought, how they were doing, how his actions or inactions would affect them.

If Dickie had had any looks about him or any money at all, none of the other boys would've stood a chance with any of the girls, including tall, handsome JR.

JR couldn't understand any of that sensitive crap. Everyone knew that this was a dog-eat-dog world and the smart person looked out for Number One. Didn't mean you needed to purposely be an asshole or go out of your way to be cruel, but JR's daddy had always told him that people needed to have opportunities to get strong, or they'd stay weak.

You did no one a favor by denying them a chance to get strong. In fact, by doing for someone what they should be doing for themselves, you were actually hurting them.

And no one wanted to hurt people.

JR's daddy had always told him if everyone looked out for themselves, and looked for ways to help themselves, then everyone could figure out how to be strong.

Strong people made for a strong country.

So when Dickie's dad had gotten sick and there was no money for medical care, JR was right there with everyone else rooting for the family- offering encouragement and moral support, but no money- Dickie's family had to figure that out for themselves. Of course, even if they had wanted to, no one in town could spare much in the way of money. Not enough to make a difference anyway.

The 'giving people the chance to help themselves' mindset made the whole issue of families in hard times a little easier to stomach; a little easier to sleep easy at night.

God loves those who help themselves and who were they to question the lessons God had to teach people?

JR slept reasonably easy at night next to his wife of a decade, Jolene. He and Jolene had known each other since 6th grade, when JR had passed her a note taped to a Moon Pie that said "I think you are the sweetest thing alive".

The next year, some of the other girls had sprouted luscious little boobies and stolen the attention of all the boys who were sprouting in their own way. So, while JR had sown his wild oats like teenage boys were supposed to do, Jolene had gone to church and waited for JR to notice her again.

When being a good girl didn't bring her any results, she'd decided to be pro-active; she was, after all, over seventeen and not engaged yet.

After the Homecoming game their senior year, Jolene made sure she was in JR's line of sight at the Friday night party in the pasture. She said a little prayer as she got into the backseat of JR's midnight blue Grand Torino, three months later she was Mrs. JR Collins, and six months after that, little JR Jr. made his debut.

Now after three more little blessings, Jolene was a little more portly, but JR thought she was still the sweetest thing alive.

He went to work, and loved his wife and his kids, and only acted the intolerable smartass when he was at Eddie's Place with the other guys…because it was expected behavior- they'd descend on the tavern after an entire day of working their asses off for bastard bosses who didn't appreciate or respect them; all the pent up frustration and anxiety that they didn't want to unleash on their wives and family ended up aimed full bore at faceless, nameless enemies.

Illegal aliens, terrorists, minorities of all genders and colors- these were easy to hate and convenient to blame, and it made them feel better to spit their venom in the general direction of these unknown but assumed assailants and then they could go home and not bite the heads off of their loved ones.

On Christmas morning and Easter Sunday he put on his dress jeans, good boots and Stetson and sat between his wife and his momma in the third pew to the left in the Little Hope Baptist Church, where the family had been going for five generations.

JR and his daddy were proud members of the local Tea Party and had been absolutely overjoyed when their candidate had actually won the presidency…and the Congress…and the Senate. *Finally* the US would get back on track, get back to the principles it was founded on- hard work, individual responsibility, freedom and God.

First order of business was to repeal the socialistic health care nightmare a previous administration had crammed down the country's throat- *finally* after 59 attempts, it was gone on the 60th.

Like a governmental ninja, of a piece they then wheeled around almost without taking a breath and cut down all those liberal commie entitlement programs that were causing the fiscal hemorrhage of the crippled nation.

Food stamps, unemployment, Medicaid, Social Security and Disability- gone.

And the people sighed in relief because now, *now* we'd see something happen- now we'd see the USA rise up again to be the greatest country in the world.

This was what they'd wanted- to 'take back' the country to a time when the savvy businessmen were rewarded and the bankers who financed businessmen were respected and every man, woman and child knew that their destiny lay solely in their own laps- all they had to do was have gumption and boot straps to pull themselves up with.

Success or the lack of it was up to each person. Anyone who was unable to achieve success just flat wasn't trying hard enough.

It first happened at the Tea Party party to celebrate the elimination of all those social entitlement programs. JR's dad had gone to the men's room and after about twenty minutes, JR noticed he hadn't come back.

The men's room was empty.

JR looked out into the parking lot- his dad's car was still there. He was still staring in confusion at the car when his phone rang.

"JR? This is Roxie at the Cum N Go- your phone number is in your dad's wallet."

"Yes? Is he OK?" JR asked, filled with dread.

"Oh, yeah- he's fine. He just wandered in about ten minutes ago and asked me what day it is. He tried to buy a candy bar, got out his wallet and just glared at it like he had no idea what to do with it. He let me take it from him to get the money out and I saw your number. Maybe you should come get him- he don't remember where he lives."

By the time JR got there, his dad was back to normal, and laughingly said he must've fallen asleep while pissing and then sleepwalked to the Cum N Go. "Snickers Hunger is a powerful thing" he said, winking.

Over the next few weeks, it happened another half dozen times, the last one causing him to actually pass out while driving, putting the front of his car through the window of the Walgreens, demolishing an entire aisle of nail polish.

The paramedics took him to the hospital as a matter of course, even though he insisted there was nothing wrong with him. At the emergency room they did a quick scan of his brain, and JR's healthy-as-a-horse dad became a cancer patient...just like that.

Once the transcriptionist typed the word 'cancer' on his medical record, his insurance company dropped him...just like that.

So the family looked at their options, which didn't take long.

JR was stewing over a brew in the back corner of Eddie's Place; he'd been there over three hours, alone. It was a Tuesday night, so slow anyway, and it was pushing closing time. Fate sighed to herself and sat down across from him after placing a fresh frosty one in front of him.

They watched the head over the amber liquid sputter and shift ever so slightly in strained and awkward companionship.

"I don't like you, JR. You're rude and selfish and a generally awful person. But you're suffering over something and you seem to have a shortage of people to talk to about it, so spill it." She leaned back in her chair and waited, impatiently impassive.

JR took a long, slow drag on the beer, frowning at her.

Talking to the glass and not her, he started out, "I just don't know anymore. I really thought we were doin' the right thing. It seemed so simple, so cut and dried- hard work and right livin' will be rewarded. All my life my daddy was the one to tell me 'everybody needs to pull their own weight' and 'gotta cut the deadwood out of the tree to save it'. But now?"

Fate's left eyebrow raised up just a bit. "Now your daddy's the deadwood?"

"It sounds fucking heartless when you say it out loud! Folks taking care of their own selves is the best way to get strong and stay free! It makes perfect sense and it's the best way to live, unless…"

"Unless it's your own loved ones who end up needing more help than your family and friends can provide" she finished his sentence gently.

"He can't die. I can't let him die. What am I gonna do?" JR whispered, now looking directly into her eyes.

And she looked directly back and directly into him. She saw him- his family and relationship with his stern and intolerant father, his difficult teenaged years always trying to prove that he was just that much tougher than any other young buck out there…he had to prove it to himself, to his dad.

She felt his dad's influence and spirit running through him- inflexible and determined, stubbornly clinging to the most black and white of life philosophies…anything that veered from the straight and narrow lane of righteousness was weak, and undeserving, and inferior.

Fate pulled the glass towards herself and took a long swig, then put it back down in front of JR.

"Baby, I'm so sorry- I got nuthin' that'll make it better. I can fix a lot of shit, but this is too big." And she patted his hand and kissed the top of his head as she walked away.

When JR caught Eddie's eye behind the bar, Eddie had grinned and sauntered over, sliding into the chair next to JR and slapping him jovially on the shoulder. They talked quietly for a bit, and then Eddie got up and walked to his office.

"I'm glad we could work something out- you're a good son, JR. A good son."

And Eddie had left the tavern with a pocket full of money after handing his soul and the title to his recently-paid-off truck over to Eddie.

He considered it a fair trade at the time.

He knew Dickie's daddy had chosen a different way, and though he felt sorry for Dickie and his family, he secretly envied them as well.

Once JR's dad had received the news of his brain tumor, he'd lashed out at his own family in fear. JR had never seen his dad afraid before. He'd turned on JR and demanded that he do something…anything that would pay for the medical bills and save his life.

"What kind of son would just let his daddy die? Any kind of a man would do whatever needed done to help his daddy out. That's how I raised you, and that's what you'd better do."

JR resisted the urge to retort with, "Maybe God is just trying to teach you something and I shouldn't interfere", but he could see where his dad's hatefulness was coming from and he said nothing except, "I'll take care of it, dad."

So JR had taken care of it and his dad was getting the treatment he needed. The only hitch was that now he was falling behind on his payments to Eddie, and Eddie had said he needed to have a little chat with him today.

Dickie had finally made it to the door, after being steadied and steered ever so slightly by Fate, and the door closed behind him. Eddie paused just a moment and then said quietly, "Come on, JR- let's take a drive."

They'd ended up in a big field outside town- the same spot all the teenagers went of a weekend night to drink beer, shoot the shit, grope their girlfriends and try to figure out that convoluted transition from childhood to adulthood.

They sat in the front seat of the truck; thick forest of tall dark pines in front of them and oddly precise square-dug stock pond behind them.

"Yer six payments behind on your loan, JR. What do you expect me to do?"

"I'm sorry, Eddie- every penny of what you gave me is gone and they're still doin' treatments- the tumor ain't quite gone yet. Every penny of my paychecks is going to the doctors right now. You understand that, right?"

Eddie smiled compassionately. "Of course I understand, brother. And I'm right glad your dad is getting better. But a deal's a deal and you gave your word. You *are* a man of your word, ain'tcha?"

"Jesus, Eddie! What do you want from me?"

Eddie pretended to think for a minute, and then said, "Well, according to our agreement, I guess I want your truck, JR."

"My truck? How the hell will I get to work without my truck, Eddie?"

Eddie's smile faded just a bit. "Not my problem, dude. Nothing personal, but we had a deal."

JR had been under a great deal of stress for a very long time. He couldn't and wouldn't accept that this was happening to him; it was as unthinkable as his dad getting cancer in the first place.

"Tell you what, asshole. I hate to give you a dirty truck. You can pick it up after I give it a good washing."

And he started the truck, slammed it into reverse, and floored it.

<u>Epilogue</u>

Fate made her way to the front of the crowd, and took in the scene in front of her.

The front grill of JR's fire-engine red Chevy Silverado crew-cab was barely above water, his naked lady chrome hood ornament seemed to be walking on the smooth surface of the stock pond; but it wasn't sinking.

The stock pond was only a few feet deep, even at the center and even after a hellacious rain storm, so there was no reason that JR and Eddie hadn't been able to get out; to just open the windows, shimmy through and walk to shore.

They'd been drunk, of course. Drunk and disoriented and they'd panicked.

Two full-grown men in a big-ass truck that'd just rolled backwards into shallow water after JR's attempt to spite Eddie had proven to have some glaring and obvious flaws, as most plans hatched in a drunken haze do.

So one had tried to climb out and slipped, briefly going head-under upside-down.

He had been frantic- possibly thought in his muddled state that the truck was rolling like a ship filling as it sank, and that caused the other one to instantly be filled with fear as well.

Her mind's eye watched in hopeless horror as the two grown men pushed each other under the surface over and over again as they tried to clamor out of the water...and then they were still.

Fate sighed, shook her head, whispered, "Fucking bird-brains," and blended back into the crowd.

BOOK THREE-

UNDEAD HUNGER-ZOMBIES FOR BRUNCH

<u>Prologue</u>

Almost gagging from the overpowering aroma of tea tree oil that permeated the rag tied over her nose, Serratia scurried quickly through the back alleys.

She hated being in here, hated the oppressive atmosphere and the overgrown tangle of neglect that the once-pristine city had become. She especially hated the mounds of maggot-infested clothing lying all around where they had fallen...the people.

Enough time had passed that everything civil and tame was going feral, but not enough for Mother Nature's clean-up crew to tidy up the fleshy leftovers.

As the virus spread and the people sickened and died, most were buried, but there were still others- mostly the poor without family or friends- who just dropped where they fell, and lay till they died.

So she averted her eyes as though they were aware of their embarrassing and compromised predicament, and thanked Gaia that as pungent as the tea tree oil was, it blocked out more than just the bacteria, but also the smell of its aftermath.

Ducking around a corner, Serratia stopped and removed a wrinkled piece of paper from her pocket. She frowned at it a minute, then stuffed it back into her worn and dirty jacket.

Being the local Healer usually meant positive perks, but every once in a while it meant she was first in line for the really shitty stuff. So now here she was, probably on a Fool's Errand right into the center of the Freak Show.

All she knew was…he'd damn well better be there.

Peering over the top of the faded red bandana tied bandito-style over her lower face, she found the building number she was looking for, glanced furtively from side to side, and disappeared into the open maw of the front door hanging askew on its hinges.

The air barely stirred and the sun beat down relentlessly. The piles of clothing moved imperceptibly as the white larvae pushed their way silently through the decaying corpses.

On the far side of the building Serratia had just been swallowed by, there was a scraping and a scratching sort of noise as a window was opened just enough to allow a body access…

..."ssshhhttthhmmmmp."

In the gutter in front of the building, a pile of leaves rustled and shifted, revealing two tiny bright and intelligent black eyes. Quick as a sneeze, the rat darted out of the gutter and into the nearest pile of clothing.

There was a brief interlude of tugging and nibbling, then the sound of Jell-O sliding reluctantly off of a spoon and the rodent popped out the other side with a 'thwack!'- slick with bodily fluids and running head high...most of a chocolate chip cookie clutched in his mouth triumphantly.

Centerville

It had all been going according to plan.

Just as had been promised, industrial towns just like Centerville had thrived after the new government took control of matters. Once the good-for-nothing lazy welfare-momma fluff was out of the national budget and the hands of the corporations were untied and set free of onerous regulations and Nanny State oversight, things really started to rock and roll.

Without having to worry about unions, minimum wages or benefits, jobs were brought back from overseas by the tens of thousands. Unemployment all but disappeared.

Without having to worry about liability insurance or inspections, production not only increased, but doubled…in some cases tripled, as the boxcars rolled in with raw materials, hit the non-stop machinery and out again- so much more streamlined without environmental restrictions, employee safety and workload limitations and quality control falderal to mess with .

It was a free market dream come true and once again the US was exploding to the top of the financial heap.

And the corporations and bankers patted the far Right politicians they'd purchased on the head and as a reward for a job well done they let them have free reign on whatever else their little hearts desired.

The Bible Belt now extended from Canada to Mexico and from sea to shining sea.

The Re-birth of America as a Shining Economic Giant was directly attributed to her long-awaited return to the Christian Values she had been founded on.

'Round about the third year into this blessed recovery, a disturbing thing started to happen.

With health care access limited to those who could afford it, only the very wealthy were getting their annual flu shots.

With the infrastructure still decimated (due to the Hammer Control and all), homes and other buildings were losing their sheltering integrity and many people lived and worked in drafty and downright dangerously cold places.

With the stress of working long hours for little pay in sometimes horrific conditions, people's immune systems sputtered, faltered, and crashed.

That winter one industrial town lost three quarters of its work force and was considering sending jobs overseas again, until they were visited by a doctor who made them an offer they couldn't resist.

Dr. Clairvius Narcisse gave the outward appearance of being the pinnacle example of humanitarian scientist.

He'd devoted his entire life to caring for the poor as long as they'd had Medicare or Medicaid (because let's face it- drugs and shit don't grow on trees), and when the poor no longer had any way to pay him, he'd started catering to the rich as could afford him, and was still happy to distribute free samples by the case to the poor working out of a dilapidated storefront on the wrong side of the tracks with a sign out front that proclaimed

Bible Study Saturdays at 1pm- lunch included

And the neighborhood folks would show up in droves to get their bible on, have a hot lunch, and if God was really in their corner, something in Dr. N's boxes would match whatever ailed them.

Sometimes it did. Sometimes it didn't.

It hurt the good doctor that he couldn't do more- he'd grown up poor himself surrounded by people just like this- it was only his good grades combined with a huge amount of luck attached to a full scholarship that pulled him out of this neighborhood, hopscotched him over the middle class subdivisions and into the gated communities of the rich.

Once there, he noticed something about the rich and their attitude towards the poor. For the most part there was a detached sort of pity and concern, but nothing more. They just couldn't relate.

Those who were born into wealth just had no idea, and those who made their way out of poverty seemed to leave it behind like a nightmare that might just pull them back in if they got too close again.

There was no evil there; just an abstract observation…like watching a play or something on TV. So it was easy for him to minister to the rich- they could afford whatever needed done, and were happy to get it and go on.

The middle class were a different story.

Whenever someone from the subdivisions came to his office, it was with great sacrifice on the part of themselves, their families, friends and sometimes the entire neighborhood. Getting the required money together to see a doctor was no small feat, and that made them angry.

They were tired from working in their middle-management jobs for low salaries and no benefits, but they couldn't relate that to what the corporations and businesses and government had done with their current situation.

Too many years of buying into the corporate lines and lingoes and promises of rewards for being 'on the same page' and aspiring to be 'team players' had taken its toll and they couldn't , they wouldn't, lay any blame on those higher up on the employment and financial food chain.

Besides, those up there were only too happy to point at someone to blame.

The poor.

The poor were takers. Lazy. Inferior. Different. Unqualified and unworthy. They were also the reason the middle class suffered so.

Dr. Narcisse cringed whenever someone of the middle class looked at him with a frustrated frown and started in…and they always did.

"Goddamn Mexicans are coming here and taking all our jobs."

"Goddamn niggers are good at working the system…just can't stand actual working."

Underneath it all was fear, of course.

Fear and the unspoken truth that those in the middle class were 100% more likely to shift downward than upward if there were any shifting to take place.

And that scared the hell out of them.

He understood that, but still couldn't tolerate it. The blatant hatred of an entire class (*his* class of birth) because of the fear of being pulled into it was something he couldn't stand and at first he tried to talk to them about it.

"Perhaps your employer should provide health insurance so you're not financially hurt by just coming to the doctor when you're sick."

"Maybe if you were paid for your overtime, you wouldn't have had to work so long and be so exhausted that you injure yourself."

This was so counter to what they had been taught that it hit them like a physical blow and they'd recoil.

"Hey, Doc- I'm just here for your medical opinion- keep your Commie Socialist crap to yourself."

So he stopped talking about it, but every day it bothered him more and more, every day he despised them more and more, and eventually it ate a hole straight through his heart.

When he approached the owners of the manufacturing plant in town with his idea, they looked at it the way any good business would- what would this do to their bottom line?

Fact was, their bottom line would love this plan. There was some initial hesitation by the more squishy of the board members, but even they couldn't deny that this was their only obvious answer to maintain the factory's solvency.

It was autumn, and the rich were getting their yearly flu shots because they could afford them without any problem. The poor just tried not to get sick, but they got sick anyway because flu germs are like that.

All the middle class knew was that some of them had seen Dr. Narcisse go into the board room on the top floor of corporate headquarters, and after he came out, there were notices up stating that the company was going to pay for flu vaccinations for all of them.

And they smiled and thought, "See? That commie bastard doctor is wrong- the company *will* take care of me!" and there was a happy sense of camaraderie as they stood in line and received their injections.

One by one they fell ill, but not with the flu, not with any one specific ailment, and not all of them... just most of them.

But the little take-home handout they had gotten said that a variety of side effects were to be expected with any vaccination sometimes, and it was OK- the company was paying for them to see Dr. Narcisse for follow-up medical care.

Dr. Narcisse had never been busier- and such a variety of symptoms- upper respiratory, urinary tract, ocular... he told them he suspected a fungal contagion and did a skin scraping on them all to rule it out.

While the cultures grew, the people who had fallen ill died; suddenly and horrifically.

The owners of the factory were as devastated as the grieving families- so devastated that they announced they couldn't go on and shut it down.

There was inquiry and testimony and the corporate executives and Dr. Narcisse and the fungal infection experts they brought in all said the same thing- the contagion had been introduced into the buildings' air vents by a family of rats who had infiltrated a small hole in the roof and then died after setting up house.

Freak coincidence, really- and nothing to do with the vaccinations…those were totally safe.

Dr. Narcisse looked up from his desk, mildly startled at the sudden appearance of the woman in front of him.

He hadn't heard the door to his office open or close, and it was a decidedly squeaky and obstinate door- he kept meaning to get it fixed but never did.

He'd been so busy treating those who had fallen ill, writing up death reports, attending funerals…really just an awful time all around and it showed in his stooped posture and look of utter and complete exhaustion…as though he hadn't slept in weeks.

So he shook his head to clear the cobwebs. Perhaps she was a trick of his eyes? No- there was a solidness about her, and he could hear her breathing and smell the aroma of Black Orchid that wafted across the room at him, invisible mists of sexuality.

He cleared his throat, half nervous and half annoyed by the interruption.

"May I help you? I don't generally see patients this late in the evening." He tried to sound professionally gruff and off-putting.

Fate just smiled at him slowly, crossed the room and had a seat in the chair in front of his desk.

"Oh, I'm not a patient, darlin'. I'm just a poor little gal who's all confused by this sad tide of sickness and death our town has been having. My mama and me think it's because we haven't been praying hard enough- what do you think?"

She looked at him sincerely, and he tried not to ogle the little church lady in front of him.

Her hair was neatly up in a sedate bun at the nape of her neck and only a few mildly disobedient tendrils refused to be harnessed – little cascades of metallic color; gold, silver, copper that were natural and not from a bottle, that was easy to see.

A single layer of black mascara adorned her big brown serious eyes flecked with green, and there was no polish on her nails. She wore no jewelry except for a single moonstone set in a silver band on the ring finger of her right hand- the hand her well-worn and dog-eared Bible was in.

A crisp pale yellow cotton blouse spattered with a tiny daisy pattern was tucked neatly into her just-below-the-knee proper denim skirt. Opaque navy tights matched the sensible Mary Janes and her legs were demurely crossed at the ankles…of course.

Nothing about her was overtly sensual, but there was something about her eyes, her full moist and natural lips, and of course the Black Orchid.

He'd never known a church lady to wear that, and his mind wondered of its own accord what else was unconventional underneath that sensible exterior façade.

Almost as if she had heard his thoughts, she smiled at him and shifted just a bit in her seat, leaned just a tad closer, and for just a moment he had a very clear view down the front of her blouse where her breasts nestled happily without the constraint of any sort of undergarment at all.

Fate whispered, "My heart is breaking for all the families of our town- please Dr. Narcisse, please help me to understand what has happened to our God-fearing community. I'm so down and scared- for the first time in my life the Good Book offers me no comfort. I'm depending on you to comfort me, Doctor."

She saw the confusion mixed with opportunity in his eyes, and he cleared his throat again.

Dr. C. Narcisse was not currently married. His third wife had left him a few months previously for the company of one of their neighbors- another doctor who had been born wealthy and didn't have the tiresome drive to help the poor people Clav (short for Clairvius) did. They were currently on their honeymoon- around the world in 80 days and taking in all the beautiful touristy sites- who wanted to see ruins and ghettos and all that mess?

With this new project for the corporation, he'd had precious little time to worry about finding any sort of female companionship. He smiled to himself to think that here it was- a gift to him apparently from God himself.

Fate watched the doctor's face and was almost disappointed that he was so easy to read.

Not that this was going to be unpleasant- Clairvius Narcisse was well-proportioned and reasonably fit. He was of average height, with short-cropped black hair and dark brown eyes. His complexion was the color of cocoa. Milk chocolate cocoa. He smelled of coffee, and fresh showered male, and something else she couldn't quite put her finger on.

Leaving her bible on the seat of her chair, she quietly moved behind the desk and knelt beside his chair, head in his lap acquiescently, one hand alongside each of his legs she pressed in ever so softly.

"Will you help me?" she whispered, warm breath disappearing into his crotch.

Without realizing it, Clav was stroking her hair- somehow he'd already undone the neat bun and the entire seat of his chair was a mass of undulating waves in shades of precious metals.

Trapped now by her hair, Fate's breath was hot and moist in his lap, and her hand gingerly yet adeptly stroked across his lap and undid his belt and the front of his pants.

He inhaled her scent and pulled her face closer in, moaning as she explored him first with her fingers, and then her mouth.

One hand on either side of her face, he guided her up onto his lap and caressed her, reached inside of her blouse and untucked it from the inside out.

They kissed slowly at first, tentatively.

While she remained just a little reserved and almost shy, he became more insistent and eager.

Fate startled and pulled back, whispering breathlessly, "I don't know if we should do this..."

Her hair had a life of its own, tickling his face, his neck his chest. His shirt was unbuttoned and her proper tights were flaccid around her ankles.

From where she was pressed against him on his lap, it was only a matter of re-positioning ever so slightly...

They gasped simultaneously- she in feigned surprise and he in sincere satisfaction, and she nestled down as deeply as she could against his rhythmic pumping.

It didn't take long at all- he'd been alone for a while and had been under more stress than he'd ever admit to.

With his final thrust, he clutched her breasts and squeezed gently yet excitedly, and she examined his fingers almost absentmindedly.

She tilted her head and covered his hands with her own- intertwining her fingers with his.

Twenty fingernails- all unadorned, yet half of them were lined with an almost invisible rim of soil. Hers were clean.

Clav let out a tremendous breath and shuddered and she remembered to gasp and exclaim in a tiny and ladylike manner, but she was focused on the fingers still intertwined. Only one had a ring on it- her moonstone set in a silver band, and she suddenly placed the aroma she hadn't been able to before...one heady scent known by many names- Angel's Trumpet, Jimsonweed, Locoweed...Moonflower.

<u>Centerville East</u>

Serratia was flummoxed, and that took quite a bit, as she'd survived this far by her quick thinking and her brass balls.

When people could no longer afford 'real' doctors, the market opened up happily to embrace a whole new field- lay practitioners.

While 'real' doctors were expensive, and the human body being what it was- twitchy and unpredictable at best- their success rate with healing or mending someone was about 75%.

Lay practitioners were a fraction of the cost, and the human body being what it was- twitchy and unpredictable at best- their success rate with healing or mending someone was about 50%.

People were only too happy to work those odds.

With times getting harder, everyone was scrambling for the extra buck, everyone was figuring out ways to make a few dollars off of their neighbors- most of the time for goods or services of equal value, but if the game was rigged just a little bit in the seller's favor...that was the way of the world, right?

Buyer beware.

People grew wary of their neighbors. They stocked up as they could on food and supplies against the economic storms, but it just wasn't something you discussed openly- why advertise what you had? That just left you open for someone to come take it.

Canned goods, paper products, cleaning supplies, over-the-counter medicines and of course weapons- guns were as always, extremely easy and cheap to buy...the NRA and gun lobby were still a leading force in the government.

It was the way of things- people didn't go out of their way to hurt each other, but if someone was in trouble more often than not they were on their own. It was expected to care for your own...nothing more.

What more could be asked in these times?

Entrepreneurship reigned supreme and the options were almost overwhelming- you could buy almost anything from anyone- food, clothing, car repair...and health care.

The key, of course, was to get someone who actually had a modicum of expertise in doctoring, and that was the tricky part.

While lots of people took money and gave out different herbs, concoctions and cures-in-a-bottle, it was pretty much a crap shoot whether or not they actually knew a damn thing about what they were doing.

After a while, in true free market style, it became marginally more apparent who had knowledge and who was clearly talking out of their ass.

Centerville East was a bustling bedroom community of Centerville; home to strip malls and decent schools, baseball fields and subdivided cul-de-sacs.

Serratia had a storefront office on a busy intersection. Her sign announced "Serratia Marcesens-Your Friendly Neighborhood Healer" halfway down the totem pole of signs identifying all the stores in a row-

GW's Liquor and Wine

Rainy Day Laundromat

(Serratia's sign)

Tiny's Sandwich Shop

Billy's Pawn

It was a one-stop shopping sort of deal.

In the way of such things, Centerville East was actually closer to the next town of size over- Middleton, than it was to Centerville. Most of the residents of Centerville East worked and did their 'big city stuff' over in Middleton, not Centerville.

The flu had hit just as hard here as in Centerville, but the major employers in Middleton were not as progressive as those in Centerville, and there was no company-sponsored vaccination program.

The healers had tried everything to stave off the flu- tinctures and teas, hand-packed capsules and poultices, but to no avail. The people of Centerville East were still getting sick with the flu.

On the one hand, some were calm enough to look at what was happening in Centerville- with people dying like proverbial flies and all, and thought to themselves, "Ya. Think I'll risk the flu itself, thanks!"

Many more only knew one thing. The flu was bad this year and they did not have access to the flu vaccine that those in Centerville did.

So they called a meeting and demanded that Someone Do Something.

<u>Centerville West</u>

Datura Inoxia held a cool rag to the child's head and softly sang a lullaby to her.

The fire in the little stove kept the small house warm against the autumn chill, and the air inside was fragranced with the simmering herbs in the little ceramic pot.

She had done all she could, and it seemed to be working. Datura had learned herb lore from the older women and like the women before her, what she knew wasn't in a book or formulary, it was in her head and her instinct helped her prescribe the various concoctions.

Most folks looked at Datura and assumed she was in her thirties…maybe forty…possibly late twenties. Hell, no one knew for sure because everyone had known her forever and she never changed.

Her jet black hair hung long and straight as an ebony waterfall, her eyes the blue water within. Her guessed heritage ranged from Native American to Irish to gypsy and back again, but no one ever asked her out loud and she never offered…just smiled and went about her business- the business of healing her people.

Centerville West was not an official suburb; when people referred to it, it was generally accompanied by a wink and a nudge.

If there had been railroad tracks, Centerville West would be on the wrong side of them.

The houses were ramshackle and the front yards were unkempt. There were no strip malls or other signs of modern civilization- on the odd corner here and there were tents set up where people brought things to trade or sell on market days.

The back yard of most homes was a patchwork quilt of vegetables, herbs and flowers and the trees in between houses were fruit and nut trees, the shrubberies were berry bushes.

The people who enforced sanitary codes and regulations had long since given up on this neighborhood and actual live chickens roamed the streets scratching and pecking up their dinners and it wasn't unusual to see a goat or three hanging out with the family dog in a fenced pen.

Children ran barefoot even in this chilly weather, wild hair flying and mismatched clothing, migrating from house to house- eating and living most anywhere and belonging to everyone.

Women and men tinkered and went about their business- the business of day to day living- in a serene and easy-going manner. They were slow to anger and quick to smile and it wasn't all from the home brew and weed, there was a sense of ease here that only comes in a place where no one cares what the clock says.

The commune had started haphazardly about twenty years prior with three families who were thinking out loud at an informal get-together.

As the economy went to hell in a hand basket the people of Centerville West pulled together, and started doing for themselves but more importantly, for each other.

Fate knocked softly on the door before entering. She was carrying a bowl of chicken soup and she placed it in front of the little girl, who smiled weakly and picked up the spoon.

While she ate, she motioned Datura to the other side of the room.

"How is she doing?" Fate looked worriedly at the small figure huddled under the blankets, surrounded by a halo of soup steam.

Datura smiled tentatively. "I think she's rounded the corner- she seems stronger and isn't as feverish."

"Good to hear, because if the rumors are true, you and I both will be very busy all too soon." Fate looked into her friend's blue eyes and their thoughts merged, trying to put together what they'd both heard and felt lately.

Even with both their thoughts melded together, the story had no real organization- nothing that made enough sense to make sense of, and they knew they'd have to go straight to the source- Rabbit.

Just the idea made them both smile and shake their heads with exasperation.

Datura left the child sleeping peacefully with her mother in attendance, and she and Fate headed to the smallest, most neglected house in the entire commune.

Bob "Rabbit" Potter was a local legend. It was said that the commune of Centerville West just sort of grew up around him, and there was no reason to doubt that.

The wilderness of his yard was a gloriously random maze of vegetables, flowers and the finest varieties of cannabis known to mankind. At the center of this (actually a little off-center, since nothing in Rabbit's world could be measured in a neat and tidy manner) was the tiny house that tilted a little off its foundation and was barely big enough to contain a plethora of smoking paraphernalia, his home-brew set-up, and as an afterthought- a bed covered in cast-off quilts of varying degrees of serviceability and cleanliness.

The women knocked once and then let themselves in.

Rabbit was sitting cross-legged on his bed, breathing deeply and staring straight ahead in meditation.

His long hair had long since gone from brownish-grey to greyish-brown and his beard stopped about mid-chest in a decidedly inconclusive way.

He was slightly built but wiry and tan, which was easy to see because he was also stark raving naked.

Standing directly in front of him, Fate said firmly but quietly, "Rabbit? You got a minute?"

"Minute, My Nut, My Newt, Mean out. Sure, I got one o' those, but only for pretty ladies such as yourselves." And he grinned at the women in a wolfish manner…a totally harmless and domesticated wolf on drugs.

Datura smiled back at him. "We hear that you've seen something outside the commune. Care to tell us about it?"

The smile disappeared and was replaced by his 'closed off I ain't sayin' nuthin' to you cops' face.

Each woman put a gentle reassuring hand on one of his shoulders. "We'll make it worth your while, Rabbit. You know we will." And the hands traced a seductive line from his neck to his wrists and back.

They knew they had a deal from his physical reaction, which was easy to tell, him being naked and all.

Fate drew a deck of playing cards out of her pocket and fanned them out in front of Rabbit's face. He tried very hard to concentrate.

"Pick a card, darlin'- any card" she said in her best street magician voice.

Rabbit picked a card and turned it over.

Queen of Hearts.

As in most decks, the cards could be read from either side, so there were actually two queens pictured- one on top and one on the bottom.

Datura handed him a joint of his best stuff and he took a long, long drag. As he did so, she said, "Now Rabbit- just concentrate real hard on that playing card. Look straight into it so hard that you are right there inside it- with the two pretty queens of hearts" and she raised his hand with the card up till it was right in between her face and Fate's face.

Rabbit exhaled and smiled. "I love me some card tricks." He looked first into Fate's brown eyes flecked with green, and then into Datura's sky blues before concentrating with all his might on the playing card.

One queen on top and one queen on the bottom.

He felt himself being gently pushed backwards onto the bed and was surrounded by the swirling fabric of their gauzy silk gypsy skirts, their hair- Fate's in colors of precious metals and Datura's as black and iridescent as the inside of a raven's eyelid, and the scent of them- Datura of fresh healing herbs and sunshine, Fate of leather and Black Orchid.

Rabbit closed his eyes in foggy ecstasy.

And they were seemingly everywhere. Stroking him, kissing him, tongues and fingers arousing him till he just couldn't stand it anymore. Reaching out he felt soft rounded hips next to his head and he buried his face into the musky softness and started kissing, licking.

And at that moment he was inside another, and she was moving back and forth, tidal and incessant, faster and faster until he came with a shudder, crying out into one and ejaculating into the other.

And he passed on everything inside him with his release- the women's minds already connected to each other saw what he'd seen.

To the west of Centerville West, deep in the forest was an abandoned factory. It'd been empty for decades, but it seemed that now it was up and running again. Probing deeper into Rabbit's admittedly easily-confused mind, they saw a fully functional facility there now, but there was something wrong with the workers.

They were moving slowly, almost mechanically, like they were in a daze or a trance.

Mentally zeroing in on individual faces, the women recognized more than a few.

The reason Rabbit had been so upset and incoherent when relaying what he'd seen to others was simple.

The workers he'd seen were the recently deceased residents of Centerville.

Fate and Datura sat silent at the little table in Rabbit's house, each holding seven cards with the balance of the deck mounded between them.

Rabbit was still caught up in the quilts and covers and last vestiges of his beautiful hallucination.

Sighing deeply, Fate asked Datura, "Got any jokers?"

Datura examined her hand. "Go fish."

Centerville East

Serratia startled at the knock on her door. Didn't those idiots know how to read? The sign said she was closed. What did a person have to do to get herself some peace and quiet?

"Go away! I'm closed!" she hollered ungraciously, then added "Unless you're really truly hurt and have cash!"

There was no answer, just another knock.

Grumbling with irritability, she yanked open the door and the two women glided smoothly past her and into the room, sitting down gracefully in a single fluid motion.

"Serratia Marcescens? The best healer in all of Centerville East?" Fate asked, her eyebrow lifted skeptically.

Serratia sized them up quickly but didn't quite know what to make of them. They were dressed like they'd just stepped out of a carnival fortune teller's tent, and the room was filled with the aroma of herbs and expensive perfume, leather and weed. Clearly they were from that Den of Imbeciles over west of Centerville, and her first impulse was to reach towards the little revolver she always kept holstered at her side and under her healer's cloak.

Because you could never be too careful.

"Oh, I wouldn't do that" Datura said conversationally, and motioned for Serratia to have a seat.

"What do you want from me?" Serratia pouted as she sat down.

"Something is happening- something big. I'm sure you've felt it, too…as a healer." Fate watched carefully for Serratia's response.

The face that won a million poker games did not flinch; in fact there was a sincere flash of anguish and sorrow as she lowered her gaze and said, "Of course. How could I not?"

Fate and Datura relaxed just a bit, and talked of the current spate of flu cases- how many had been sickened, how many had died, and the best ways to try to strengthen the bodies to overcome the virus.

Serratia was totally lost in all the herbal natural gobbledygook they were yammering at her. She'd barely graduated high school and had been a clerk at the Walgreen's since she was 16, and had for years made a tiny side income from skimming a few painkillers here, a few narcotics there.

When the whole 'lay practitioner' thing had started up, she saw her opportunity and grabbed it with both hands- emptying the pharmacy bit by bit of antibiotics and other shit she thought may be helpful till she had a solid and impressive stockpile; with no pharmaceutical regulations, no one kept track of missing pills and syrups.

Right now her main worry wasn't how to help people get better; it was keeping that bitch Vibrio Cholerae from stealing her place as the best healer in Centerville East.

Outwardly she was listening with rapt attention to everything Fate and Datura were telling her- but inside she was replaying the last town meeting over and over in her head.

When the townspeople had demanded Someone Do Something they had all naturally looked to her, but before she could even manage a sincerely humble smile and stand to speak, there was that god-awful fingernails on a chalkboard voice of Vibrio's...crapping on her parade from the back of the room.

"I can fix it! I've been looking through the books of the healers and I know how to concoct a cure!" Vibrio was gleefully leering at Serratia.

The entire room turned to look at Vibrio and she was commissioned to come up with a full report and get back to the people within 72 hours.

That was 24 hours ago, and Serratia still had no fucking idea how to pull attention back where it belonged...on herself.

Snippets of what the two ridiculous women were going on about were getting through to her- something about bacteria-contaminated flu vaccines...blah blah blah...skin scrapings that really infected the patients with the venom from a puffer fish or toad or some such stupid shit...blah...blah...blah...death that wasn't really death...blah...blah...blah...digging up the bodies and dosing with a drug that made the people compliant and slow, not able to do anything but what they were told to do...blah...blah...blah...a factory in the forest? These gals really had been tokin' it up, hadn't they?

Wait. What?

"Flu vaccine".

Datura stopped mid-sentence and frowned. "I'm sorry? What?"

Serratia looked excited and repeated it. "Flu vaccine? Did you say someone somewhere has flu vaccine to sell?"

Fate looked at her intently. "Yes. Dr. Narcisse in Centerville is the one who's been vaccinating all the company workers there."

Datura was quick to add, "But, you don't want that stuff! It's been *ouch*!" as she was kicked smartly on the shin under the table.

"What do you mean I don't want it? Of course I want it! Do you realize how rich it will make me? I...ummm...I mean, how many of my people would be helped by it? All of them! All of them." And she mentally added up what she could charge for the vaccine times the number of people in Centerville East.

"Dr. Clairvius Narcisse in Centerville is the man you need to see for that. I've met him. He's a very nice man and I'm sure you'll be able to work something out that will benefit you both. And your people, of course." Fate smiled warmly.

"Well, so much for recruiting another healer to help us- looks like we're on our own" Datura observed as they made their way back to Centerville West.

"You and I are enough, darlin'. It would've been nice to have help, but we're more than enough. Just ask Rabbit." And they both laughed.

"Although I do feel a little guilty- poor Serratia thinks she needs to watch her back for Vibrio? Wait till she meets Karma." And Fate and Datura both laughed and didn't really feel guilty at all.

<u>West of Centerville West</u>

It had taken them only a day of watching the factory, but Fate and Datura now knew the routine of the place. It was pretty simple, because the people now there were pretty simple.

Every morning they gathered for their meager breakfast of weak coffee and some sort of gruel, laced with the drug that would keep them hostage in their own bodies.

They were allowed an hour outside in the sunshine (or rain, or cold- it really didn't matter since they just…sat until it was time to go back inside). During that hour it was not unusual for one or two of the workers to wander off, veer off-course a bit and careen out of sight.

At first the women wondered why no one went after them, but after further investigation they realized that there was an actual moat around the entire place- with very steep sides not so much to keep the victims from climbing out as to keep the alligators in. But it all worked together.

If a worker was injured on the job, they were unceremoniously dumped into the moat.

Because there would always be more bodies.

With the help of a simple sapling foot bridge, the next few lunch hours Fate and Datura would cross over and wait. As the wanderers veered off-course, they were intercepted by one of the women, who gently steered them across the bridge to safety.

Unsure of how to reach the hapless workers while still under the power of the drug, they decided to appeal to the most basic instinct in all of us.

Once away from the factory and the mind-altering daily dose of drugs, the people slowly regained some of their previous memories and mental faculties- a few were able to remember enough to recall names of their relations and these were surreptitiously contacted and the entire family relocated into the maze of Centerville West.

But getting them to follow on their own could be problematic.

The man turned a blank face towards Fate. He looked straight through her on the way back into his head, but there was nothing there for him to focus on- every complex thought process was blocked, buried, just out of his reach.

Fate put one hand on either side of his face and stroked his dirty cheeks gently.

Leaning in closer to him, close enough for her to feel the beating of his heart against her breasts, she breathed three little words into his ear and there was a spark of recognition in his eyes, a flash of desire.

"Are you hungry?"

<u>Centerville</u>

This was not going as smoothly as she had planned.

Serratia had waited in that filthy room for an eternity before the doctor had finally shown up.

He was carrying a large padded envelope; she could see the bubble wrap liner peeking out from under the plain brown paper. Inside the envelope was her ticket to fortune- twenty 100ml vials of flu vaccine.

She was purchasing it for $20 per cc and would sell it for $120 per cc.

$40,000 in cash was bundled neatly inside her jacket- all the cash she had had on hand and all the cash she could amass quickly in back alley poker games and pushing out-of-date drugs on desperate people.

She was momentarily happily surprised at how handsome the doctor was. She should've known, since that whore Fate had winked and grinned when she'd said he was a 'very nice man'. In other times and circumstances Serratia would've been happy to bring him home, open up and let him dip into her a time or two...for a price, of course.

But this was much bigger than that, and she had money to make and that bitch Vibrio to show up. No one was going to steal her thunder.

"Do you have the money?" the doctor wasted no time on small talk.

"Of course. $40,000 as agreed" and she started to take the money out of her jacket.

"$100,000" the doctor said calmly.

Serratia saw red. "You nigger son-of-a-bitch!" she screamed. "I saw the sign on the door- you treat these ghetto rats for free and you want to cheat good hard-working middle class people out of something they need to save their lives?"

Serratia was very good at being righteously indignant when it was in her best interests.

He struck her so hard with the back of his hand she felt one of her teeth loosen in its socket. Maybe two. Blood trickled out of her mouth from where her own teeth had cut into her lip.

Dr. Clairvius Narcisse had always been a patient man, a kind man, a gentle man. He'd been dragged by life to the very end of his rope and had managed to hang on until now.

He looked down at this charlatan whose only goal was to take care of herself. She was a member of the class who irrationally and outright hated the people who had raised him, loved him, cared for him, and birthed him- his people.

He felt a small acknowledgment that she hated her own people as well- if she couldn't make a buck off of them, she didn't care what happened to any of them.

All his life he'd been trained to heal and to cure, to 'First do no harm' but he was over that now.

And now he was going to kill her.

Epilogue

Serratia flinched as the hand came towards her again, but it didn't connect.

She gasped, and realized that the air was no longer putrid, but laced with the scent of Black Orchid. Tentatively, she opened her eyes.

The doctor lay in a quickly widening pool of his own blood and he stared fixedly and with some consternation at the ceiling. Somewhat distractedly, she thought it would've served him better to be considering the huge hole in his chest where his heart used to be- the ceiling had had nothing to do with his death.

The hand now extended towards her was warm, and firm, and strong- adorned with a simple ring set with a moonstone.

Fate's eyes sparkled at her and she said, "It's alright now- no one will bother you on your way home."

The package held tight to her, her $40,000 still inside her jacket, Serratia whispered, "Thank you!" and was gone in a blink.

Fate waited just a moment, then couldn't stand being in the same room with the dead doctor one minute longer. Now that there was no one to administer the 'death-inducing' toxin, or the drug to keep the recently-deceased compliant, those already under its spell would recover, at least somewhat.

Of course, all of the people Serratia vaccinated would be infected with the bacterium that would make them sick with a variety of ailments, but most of them would recover, unlike her dubious reputation as a healer.

Skirting around the maroon puddle that he now seemed to float in, she casually reached into her pocket, pulled out the doctor's heart and considered it for a moment- turning it this way and that to examine all sides of it.

"Such a shame. It started out to be a good heart, a tender heart- I just can't see where it went wrong. "

She shook her head sadly and tossed it aside, closed the door behind her and strolled out into the sunlight.

There was a rustling in the gutter and a rat still slick with slime skittered across the lawn, up her pants leg and onto her shoulder.

"A cookie? How sweet!" Fate smiled fondly at the rodent and took a bite.

Postscript

My apologies to those zombie fans who are now shaking their heads and saying out loud, "That was *bull*shit. She don't know zombies from a hole in her ass."

True zombie aficionados caught onto it early on…round about page nine with the introduction of the good doctor.

So, no- there were no zombie hoards lurching around just waiting for some guys with AK47's to blow their heads off before they inexplicably eat the brains of innocents…because what's better than an unlimited number of shuffling slow unarmed targets, am I right?

Here's what I think, though. The truly scary shit is stuff that could conceivably happen if everything lined up just right.

So let me introduce our cast of characters.

Serratia Marcescens is a bacterium that actually made its way into the flu vaccines one year…by accident, of course. It made a lot of people sick with a weird variety of ailments and even killed a few.

Clairvius Narcisse was a Haitian who had the dubious distinction of being zombified by a voo doo witch doctor, who'd been paid by Clairvius' brother because he was pissed off at him. The good witch doctor was already doing a brisk business zombifying citizens and selling them to a sugar plantation as laborers.

The basic recipe was to introduce the toxin from either a puffer fish or buffo toad via skin abridement- basically a skin scraping. This would cause the victim to get really sick and 'die'- Clairvius was examined by two American doctors who both pronounced him dead. This was in 1961, so…ya. Not back in the dark ages.

Once 'dead' the victim was buried and then dug up again, revived and kept in a state of forgetful compliance by daily dosages of

Datura Inoxia, also known as Loco Weed by ranchers. When livestock eat it, they lurch around stiff-legged and apparently blind. If they eat too much of it, they die.

Vibrio Cholerae? A bacteria spread by fecal matter…just because someone needed to be there as Serratia's pain in the ass.

A final word about the first words in the story.

Tea Tree Oil really will block and/or kill many germs, including Serratia Marcescens.

It's not that I *couldn't* write that other more gory, violent and brain-matter-spewed scenario, because I totally could.

I just tend to be more afraid of things that really *could* happen, and what more proof of that than something that already has?

BOOK FOUR-

DON'T FORGET THE BULLET LUBE

Prologue

Time seemed to stand still, just like in the movies.

He could hear the blood pounding in his own ears; imagined the never-ending coursing of the red fluid through his veins from one end of his body to the other, felt the pumping of his heart pushing it onward for another round, ever onward.

He wanted to remember this moment forever- the way the sunlight filtered and flashed through the leaves of the trees, turning everything in the forest into glitter and disco, simulated slow motion.

This was it.

All the years of training and practicing, thousands of rounds of ammo spent at the Range, and it all came down to this one shining moment.

A shadow fell over his thoughts just briefly, the very briefest of doubts…was this the right thing to do?

He shook his head in disgust with himself. This was not the time for thinking, and he was not a thinking man, no how.

He was Tig Carroll, born and raised right here in these woods, just like every generation before him were.

Short and wiry, lean and spare, Tig was the absolute spitting image of every other Carroll in the area, ever.

None of them had ever been accused of being big thinkers.

Good workers, hard drinkers, devout church-goers (They'd made a deal with the Almighty years ago- they'd attend church with their wimmen-folk on Sunday if He looked the other way the other days of the week. So far, so good), and all of them tits deep in the culture of the bible belt- the gun culture.

Tig felt the cool rough bark of the Loblolly pine against his cheek, his chest, his leg...steadying him for the shot.

He inhaled the good clean aroma of pine and sand, water and heat of the air that had filled his lungs for all of his 34 years- he'd never taken a breath outside of this county.

This was it.

He snugged the rifle butt even closer in than it already was, calming at the familiarity of it.

Out of all his collection, this was the one he'd chosen for today- because what other one would have been better for a stealth mission such as this?

Stealth was the name of the game with the BAR LongTrac Stalker.

This rugged and powerful auto-loading rifle was capable of delivering magnum-level power with pinpoint accuracy.

From its matte black alloy receiver and hammer-forged barrel to its multi-lug bolt, this BAR was ready to put rounds right on target over and over again, without pause.

The BAR LongTrac Stalker was the hunting rifle that set the bar for every other autoloader on the planet.

There was movement up ahead- his quarry came into sight, and Tig felt the pleasurable stirring in his loins that always preceded pulling the trigger.

That was only natural, right?

He pushed back the last shred of doubt and took a deep breath. This had to be done- the country was going to hell in a hand basket and this was the only thing that would fix it, no matter anyone's personal feelings on the matter.

The President said so. The Preacher said so. God said so...according to the President and the Preacher.

He was a proud American and a good Christian and it was time.

This was it.

He sighted in on his prey, who just then turned his head and looked directly at him, without seeing him, and it registered just for a second that it was like looking into a mirror.

As he squeezed the trigger, Tig heard the voice of his old Sunday school teacher, Ms. Libby buzzing in his ear- lining up all the boys for a photograph and clucking, "You Carroll boys all look exactly alike, cut from the same cloth and all peas in a pod..."

<u>Down at the Church</u>

Not a head turned and the preacher never skipped a beat, but everyone was aware of the stranger as she silently slipped into the back pew.

Tiny country churches were known for their charity, their kindness and their Christian acceptance…for everyone in their own tiny flock. Anyone from 'outside' was fully suspect and to be watched carefully.

Anyone who was anyone knew this rule of tiny country churches, so visitors were a rare occurrence- so rare that mothers and fathers had to poke their children several times while scowling in disapproval. The children had never seen anyone in church that they hadn't known their entire lives.

And yet, there she was, big as life and sitting right between old Mr. Milner and the aisle.

Mr. Milner was mostly blind, nearly deaf and only half the time remembered where he was at any given moment. Being as he was also well over ninety years old, this was to be expected.

What wasn't expected was his outburst in church this morning.

"God DAMN, someone smells good!"

Maybeth Milner, Mr. Milner's spinster granddaughter, was sitting on the other side of him. "Shhhh...Granddad."

The stranger sat still and serene- head bowed devoutly, she pretended not to hear Mr. Milner. She wore a pale lavender sun dress, and a light peach crocheted shawl around her shoulders gave the dress 'church-worthiness'.

Her well-worn bible rested in her lap and her low-heeled sandaled feet crossed at the ankles demurely.

Her head was bowed, and although some of her hair was pulled back in a nice conservative barrette, most of it still managed to cascade forward to screen her barely-contained smile in a luxuriant flurry of precious metallic hues.

"She's here, ain't she? Lorrene! I can explain!" The entire congregation turned around curiously at Mr. Milner's entreaty to his long-dead wife.

Maybeth leaned across her grandfather and apologized in a stage-whisper to the woman. "I'm so sorry- he forgets things and places and can be very inappropriate sometimes."

The woman just nodded and patted him on the knee reassuringly, whispering in return that she understood and it was quite alright.

Her hand remained on his knee.

Maybeth turned gratefully back to her hymnal after giving the rest of the congregants a 'what are ya'll still looking at?' glare and everything returned to normal.

Fate continued to look intently at the bible in her lap but in her mind's eye she was far away in Mr. Milner's brain.

He had been newly married and so very young when he shipped overseas. That year he'd graduated high school, married Lorrene wearing his brand new uniform and left her here at home with Maybeth's momma in her tummy- a souvenir of their weekend honeymoon to Branson Missouri- all in the course of three months.

It had been his duty, of course, and he was right proud to do it. He just hadn't been prepared for the strangeness of everything, the unfamiliarity of everyone... and that was before leaving this shore for a foreign one.

Once over yonder they may as well have dropped him on a different planet.

Everything was an assault.

The air was weird, the food was unrecognizable, the people were strange, the noises incomprehensible.

He was never alone and it was never quiet- he'd never been part of a teeming mass of humanity before.

The cacophony was overwhelming.

The smell was overpowering.

The loneliness was almost too much to bear.

He headed to the whore house with the rest of his buddies, but only because it was expected of him.

The women were not much older than girls, but the men were not much more than boys, so in some twisted, unnatural way it all evened out.

They could make more in the whorehouse than their entire family could make otherwise- especially with so much of their country occupied by foreigners and having the shit bombed out of it, so there they were.

He was shy, yet curious and she was reasonably pretty and businesslike. She had long...everything- hair, legs, eyelashes, even her tongue- and she smelled and tasted of flowers and spices, sandalwood and musk.

It was the only time he would 'step out' on Lorrene in their entire 70+ year marriage, and he hadn't smelled anything like that since.

Until today, when Miss Fate Devine sat next to him in the little church wearing her best Sunday Go to Meeting clothes and her Black Orchid perfume.

Mr. Milner was quiet and well-behaved again- his thoughts were turned inward as he recalled that girl far away and years ago and what she could do with that long, slippery serpentine tongue; things that a country boy from rural America had never even thought about... and he had just the hint of a smile on his face as Fate patted his knee again and turned her attention to the sermon.

The sermon was why she was here in the first place. She'd heard Brother Louis gave a helluva sermon.

Since the new government had taken over, people tended more and more to just get their current event news, political opinions and soul-saving all done in one place- at church.

It was easier, it was quicker, and it was encouraged- now that there was no separation of church and state, what more perfect place to get everything than in God's House?

God's chosen people gathering together in His house in this glorious land that He'd blessed them with…what could possibly be better?

Well, actually quite a bit could be better.

The country was still in trouble; in fact it was sinking deeper and deeper into poverty, neglect and despair every single day- people were unable to make a living wage and they were constantly getting sick or hurt from the conditions they had to work in or the foods and products they had to consume that went completely without oversight now.

It was a total mystery.

They'd done everything right- they'd cut social programs till they didn't exist anymore to balance the budget and encourage people to be responsible citizens, they'd given corporations and banks totally free rein to bring all the jobs and prosperity back, and they'd put God front and center of everything everywhere- and not just any old god, but the God of the Christian Bible...just as the Founding Fathers intended.

There was only one answer.

They still weren't doing enough.

They needed more austerity, more free market, more devotion- if all they had done wasn't working; they just needed more of the same.

Nothing else made sense or could possibly save them.

There had to be something somewhere somehow that had been missed- something they were doing or not doing that was causing displeasure on God's part.

Fate listened to the familiar screed and almost dozed through the punch line.

Pastor Louis announced that the Men of God and the Men of Government- now blessedly the same men- had all had a come to Jesus Meeting and Jesus had spoken to them. The reason America was still faltering?

The Gays.

The bible in her lap suddenly seemed way too heavy a burden and Fate left it on the pew next to Mr. Milner as she quietly but quickly exited the church.

Up at the Range

After church, all the women and children went home to start Sunday dinners and the men took themselves to the Range to discuss the sermon and other forms of current events.

No man left home without his Bible or his gun(s) on any day of the week, but most of all on Sundays.

The preacher was there, too, of course. Sans clerical collar he looked like any other man there- comfortable flannel shirts over well-worn Wranglers, scuffed and worn work boots below and some sort of dented and sweat-covered headwear above made up the uniform of the Real American Male.

Range time was much more than gun-cleaning and ammo-loading and target-shooting. It was for all intents and purposes After-Church; time for the men to discuss current events and what they could do as individuals to help their great country keep healing herself after almost a decade of liberal decadence, selfishness and evil almost completely destroyed Her.

Today's sermon was fresh on everyone's mind, even as Tag Carroll took his new gun out of the truck to show off to his buddies. It was just like Tig's favorite, and Tag had been crazy wanting one for a good while. This past week had been his 20th wedding anniversary and God bless his wife- she knew just what to get him.

She'd saved up for a year from her grocery allowance, going without her own little bit of makeup and face cream and shorting the kids' lunches so she could surprise him with it. What a woman! He was so blessed.

Actually, all the Carroll boys had made good marriages so far. Momma Carroll had had five boys- Tag, Tye, Tommy, and the twins Tig and Tucker.

Everyone but Tucker had been married off young and had a passel of kids- and all were active in the church community, being raised up Soldiers for Jesus and American Patriots.

They'd milled around for a bit after arriving at the Range, talking about the sermon they'd all heard that morning.

That being gay was a sin wasn't questioned *at all*- everyone knew it just wasn't natural- to lust after anything but your sweet docile wife's soft and welcoming vagina was not allowed; to lust after another penis or anything resembling your own plumbing was complete anathema.

Tig wasn't there yet and Tag was showing off his anniversary gift to the admiring audience, who watched him with quiet envy and barely concealed desire for the beauty of the thing.

"Looka here", Tag had the gun cradled in his arm tenderly. He stroked the barrel slowly, eyes half-closed he recited the features of the rifle from memory. "This here hammer-forged barrel provides outstanding strength, lasting durability and precise accuracy."

"The barrel's target-type Crown" (running a fingertip across the tip of the muzzle in a slow, circular motion) "enables a uniform release of gas as the bullet exits the muzzle, and that helps prevent any unwanted shift in bullet trajectory. The barrel Crown is recessed to help protect it from accidental impact damage that can degrade accuracy."

One man broke the silence by interjecting, "Well, if you wouldn't keep dropping yer gun, you wouldn't have to worry about that!" and there was good-natured snickering and elbowing.

Tag never even paused; his eyes never left the beautiful Browning in his arms.

"The matte black aircraft grade alloy receiver on this baby is drilled and tapped for scope mounts to provide a rock-solid optics mounting platform- that'll really get your load exactly where you want it."

"This is a gas-operated autoloader with a high-strength multiple lug rotating bolt that locks directly into the barrel. See here?"

"The seven-lug bolt and precise breech-to-chamber relationship give it exceptional accuracy and the strength to handle modern magnum class cartridges."

Just then his cell phone rang and he answered it with hushed and quiet annoyance.

"Tig? Why ain't you here yet? Yep, sure- bring those new loads you want tested...come on. And Tig? Don't forget the bullet lube." He turned his attention back to the rifle.

"See this? It's gotta strong, rigid action bar block link-up- that improves accuracy by reducing barrel vibration. Strong, long and solid- that's what this is."

Point by point Tag went over the rifle inch by inch, and the men watched rapt in the beauty of it and their eyes followed his fingers playing along the barrel, the stock, the trigger...over and over again.

The buffering mechanism to reduce wear and stress on the rifle's mechanism for longer life and greater reliability- you could fire this baby off time after time and it'd never let you down.

The bolt release lever incorporated in the receiver for maximum reliability and ease of access, even when wearing gloves. Because sometimes you just need gloves for better control and comfort.

The floorplate was hinged, allowing access to the detachable box magazine for quick and easy loading and unloading, meaning less waiting between firing off.

The trigger design provided a crisp pull that broke like a glass rod and they all caught their breath simultaneously at the beautiful sharpness of it.

The generous trigger guard opening allowed for easy access…again- even when wearing gloves.

The stock and metalwork were intended to shrug off every day wear and reduce game-spooking reflections, because nothing was more maddening and disruptive to a good hunt than spooked game. Nothing was as frustrating as setting up your shot, getting your equipment all in place and your trigger finger primed and then *poof*- your target is gone and your left with nothing but your weapon in your hand.

The charging handle on the bolt was sculpted to give a solid grasp without snagging on clothing or rifle scabbard. This baby was smooth as a baby's behind from end to end.

The crossbolt safety offered easy accessibility without removing your firing hand from the stock. You could quickly manipulate the safety, or verify the position of the safety, without losing your sight picture or cheek weld- and concentration is key to a successful and pleasurable shooting outcome.

The Composite buttstock was user-adjustable for cast-on, cast off and drop at comb via interchangeable shims that inserted smoothly as needed between the stock and the receiver to facilitate the inevitable adjustments needed depending on the situation.

The men gathered around and admired the over-molded panels on the pistol grip and fore-end. All agreed it would improve your grip, and be really appreciated when using the gun in adverse or wet conditions.

The well-formed recoil pad had optional interchangeable pads to allow for adjusting the length of pull and greatly reduce felt-recoil and flinching. None of them would admit to flinching when pulling the trigger, but... *some* guys might.

Sling swivel studs were pre-installed for easy mounting of the sling.

And if there was one thing that made for a truly enjoyable and fulfilling shooting experience...it was an easily mounted sling.

Overall, this baby would be the one to go to for most any hunt; the one that'd never let him down and keep on keeping on all day long under any circumstances.

Tag Carroll continued to stroke the Browning and murmured to himself as much as to anyone else present, "Yep- this is a beauty. And the best thing about it? It ain't just a gorgeous deer hunting rifle. It's a kick-ass sniper rifle."

And all the men smiled and nodded silently...point taken.

Of course no one would say it out loud, but as Americans, and Christians, who loved their country and their God, they knew that someday, sometime, somehow...they may be forced to protect themselves or their families against an enemy of the state or anyone who threatened the moral fiber of their immediate area by having unnatural feelings towards anything but a female spouse.

And no one would blame them at all.

Self-defense. Protecting their loved ones.

Standing their ground.

Over at the Courthouse

The woman tapped politely on the door, and waited patiently till the Sheriff looked up from his newspaper.

His practiced look of pained courtesy was usually enough to send most people apologizing and beating a hasty retreat, but he froze mid-look when he saw how damn attractive this visitor was.

Backlit in the doorway, her hair seemed to move on its own in shades of silver, gold and copper; waves of softness framing her serious face and contained only by the black-framed reading glasses perched atop her head.

Wearing a simple matching skirt and jacket in a light spring tweed, the skirt ending just at her knees and the jacket open to reveal the raw silk blouse underneath- the first three buttons undone.

The scent of Black Orchid preceded her into the office and she sat down smoothly and silently across from him, catlike.

She lowered her glasses and read from a small notebook in her hand. "Sheriff Thomas?" she glanced up at him, her brown eyes flecked with green magnified in her lenses. He nodded.

"May I ask you a few questions?" and she pushed the glasses back onto her head, smiled, and sat back in the chair, clearly going nowhere no matter what his answer was going to be.

As she sat back, her blouse opened up just a bit, revealing a glance of cleavage.

Sheriff Smith Thomas was a quick thinker- that's what'd kept him alive all these years in law enforcement, in life and in his decades-long marriage to Ginny.

He and Ginny had grown up together and their families were best friends together. Any other ending other than being married to one another had never crossed the minds of anyone in either family, including themselves.

Sheriff Thomas cleared his throat, and answered gruffly, "Well, maybe just a few…as you can see, I'm a very busy man. What is this for, Mrs….?"

"Oh, I'm so sorry. It's Miss. Miss Fate Devine, and I'm writing a book on lawmen of the South- such a noble and disappearing breed." She flushed at the thought, and his predatory instincts took over.

"Miss Devine. I do have just a short spell here where I can talk with you. What would you like to know?"

She asked him about his motives for becoming a law enforcement officer, how long he'd been Sheriff, and for a few anecdotal stories from his days on patrol. The answers rolled off of his tongue effortlessly- he'd been asked the same thing by everyone from news reporters to 3rd graders and it took no thought at all, which gave him ample time to admire her as she wrote- head bowed, glasses on again, hair shielding her face and framing her long slender neck. He watched the steady rise and fall of her bosom and knew right then where this interview was going to end up.

As though reading his mind, Fate looked up and over the top of her glasses and smiled. "I'm so very sorry- I'm sure I'm intruding on your suppertime."

"Not at all- always happy to be of assistance to fans of law enforcement." And he called home and told Ginny he'd be late... something had come up. She told him to be careful and she'd keep his dinner warm for him. The house sounded quiet. It was always quiet at home.

Fate tilted her head as he hung up and continued her questions on different threats to society as he saw them.

They included the usual suspects- drunks, druggies, sociopaths, minorities, illegals…terrorists weren't such a threat in this little Southern town but you just never knew and had to keep your eyes open. Fate paused for a moment in thought.

"How about what I've been hearing lately? How about the Gays?"

Smith never even paused. "I think the government and the churches have it right- we've overlooked the Gays as a threat for far too long. As far as I'm concerned, they'd better just repent and find Jesus like any other good American instead of being unnatural sinners. We've come a long ways as a country in the last few years to counteract the evil liberal Socialism that tried to take hold, but it's not enough. God is still judging us and I can see where the Gays have a lot to do with it."

There was a moment of silence.

Her pen tapped on her notebook; staccato and insistent. She seemed hesitant.

"Sheriff Thomas? What if one of your children came to you and told you they were gay?"

Smith frowned at her. "Well, Missy. That just isn't a problem in these parts- we raise our young'uns right here."

"But, just for the sake of argument? Just a 'fer instance'? What would you do if your own child came to you and told you they were gay?"

Sheriff Thomas pulled himself up to his full height behind the desk and looked sternly down at her. "Miss Devine- I've told you how I feel on this matter. We've been assured by our preachers and our government that the Gays are destroying America and it is the official opinion of law enforcement that anyone who feels threatened by the advances of a homosexual will be expected to Stand Their Ground as a matter of morals and personal safety."

"As for your questions regarding my own family, my wife and I have no children. The Good Lord saw fit to not bestow the blessing of offspring upon us, which has hurt my wife deeply and enduringly. Now if you please, let this topic lie."

Fate looked up at him through glasses and hair and he saw tears glimmering in her eyes. "I'm so sorry- I

184

didn't mean to be hurtful. That was never my intent."

On the outside it looked like Smith's defenses were completely undone. Inside his head he was smiling at how ridiculously easy this was going to be.

"Miss Devine- I never meant to be rude and I'd like to make amends. May I buy you dinner?"

On the outside it looked like Fate was contritely grateful. Inside her head she was smiling at how ridiculously easy this was going to be.

"Why, thank you Sheriff Thomas. I have a room at the Sheraton over in Nashville- would you be interested in a quiet room service meal?"

One hour later, Smith Thomas knocked on the door of room 215 and Fate answered it. He was still in uniform, but she had changed her clothes. She still wore her raw silk blouse, but had abandoned her bra and exchanged her jacket and skirt for satin pajama pants.

The door closed behind them.

Neither one of them made any mention of dinner.

The king sized bed was well-appointed and the sheets turned down, and Smith stood just inside the door as she divested herself of first the blouse, then the satin pants. There was nothing underneath them.

"Sheriff? Are you going to guard the door all night, or come keep me company?" she smiled.

He laid his uniform neatly on a chair beside the bed- folded and right-side out, in the order they'd be put back on. Sheriff Thomas had always been a quick thinker and had learned what it took to not only survive, but make sure he never got caught.

He laid his Glock .40 on the bedside table, facing away from them, but angled for quick and easy access if needed.

Sex had always been a pretty straightforward affair for Smith. He enjoyed the chase, relished the catch, and knew he was supposed to be all about the big finish. He assumed that it was his strict religious upbringing that caused the big finish to just not hold much appeal to him, but he'd always secretly wondered at the lack of a finish at all most of the time.

He'd assured Ginny it wasn't her fault because it wasn't. Ginny was a fine Christian woman, not hardly hard on the eyes, and willing as the day was long…mainly because she'd always wanted children so desperately.

Fate was lying on the bed completely naked and beautiful, one eyebrow raised. "If you're busy, Smith- we can do this later…"

Smith's face got red and he started to get angry, then chuckled in spite of himself and pulled back the covers.

Fate sighed inwardly at the awkward confidence of Southern Fundamental Baptist men as Smith climbed on top of her without so much as a handshake or kiss on the cheek.

She could've rolled her eyeballs because his eyes were closed, but she resisted the impulse.

He was inside her and just going to town rhythmically, eyes closed in concentration and effort, and she wrapped her legs around his and made little cooing noises- just enough to express pleasure, but not enough to sound like a slutty heathen.

It flummoxed her at first that these men could so easily accept that they were so much God's keepers and stewards of the Earth that it was just natural for any woman to spread their legs for them to accept their Blessed Seed…women were only whores if they spread their legs for other men and *not* them.

After an interminable fifteen minutes (she timed it using the alarm clock on the table), Smith was still pumping but losing his erection, and sweat was falling from his face onto hers in large depressed droplets.

She cried out politely but passionately (enough), gently grabbed his shoulders and steered him off of her so that he was lying with his back to her- almost gasping for air from his exertion.

She snuggled up close behind him, draping her arm over his side and stroking his chest. "I think I know what will help," she whispered into his ear.

He felt her behind him- her metallic locks tangling against his neck, her breasts soft and pillow-like against his back, and he relaxed and just let her slender hand play up and down his chest.

He was almost asleep when he looked down and noticed the change in her hand. It seemed bigger, the fingers more squared-off and the nails shorter. He could've sworn she'd been wearing a ring.

He put his hand on her forearm and felt a wiry covering of hair. His neck was no longer tangled in her long tresses, but being tickled by a short, neatly trimmed beard.

Her breasts were nowhere to be felt, replaced by thick curly chest hair sticking to his sweaty back.

Before his tired mind could fully process all this, her pelvis pushed gently forward and first the bulbous end, followed by a fully erect penis smoothly slid into his anus completely and he felt a satisfying nestling of firm testicles against his buttocks.

His sphincter contracted almost violently and he spilled his Blessed Seed onto the sheet in front of him with a shudder and a cry.

Simultaneously, her hand shrank back into its feminine shape, her moonstone ring glowed in the light of the single lamp, and his neck was entangled in the fullness of her hair again, her breasts pushed up against his back and he felt her breathing heavily from her own climax.

Semen leaked out of his anus and mixed with his own in a sticky river of truth.

"Well, well, well, Sheriff. I think we now know why poor Mrs. Thomas is childless, don't we?" she whispered not unkindly in his ear, and his heart froze in his chest with confusion, fear and white hot anger.

"We're not all alike, Smith. Just because someone is different doesn't make them evil. Your god made us all in his image, remember?" Her breath was warm on his neck.

Without thinking, his Glock was in his hand and he flipped over to face her, firing one shot where her brown eyes had been.

Sheriff Smith Thomas was alone in the bed, save for the Gideon's Bible that now had a bullet hole right through the 'o' in Holy.

Off the Deep End

Tig Carroll felt like someone had punched him in the stomach. In fact, that would've been far preferable to this mental turmoil...the Carroll boys were not good at mental turmoil.

When he'd driven to Tucker's house he'd been so certain the drive home would be better; he'd be smiling and reassured and feeling just a little silly that the conversation behind him would have even occurred at all.

It all started with the phone call from the preacher, asking Tig if he'd be willing to take over the Boy Scout troop leadership at the church.

"I don't understand- Tucker's been the troop leader since he was 18...over fifteen years now. The scout troop is his life." If Tucker had decided to quit, he would've told Tig about it- they were twins- they told each other everything.

So Tig had gone to the church and sat uncomprehending as the preacher told him why Tucker could no longer be the troop leader. "Surely you can see why" the Preacher had said, frowning.

Tig frowned back, sincerely. He had no idea why Tucker was being asked to step down and he said so.

"Tig, seriously? We've ignored this for years because Tucker's a good scout leader and the boys all love him. But in light of everything we're now being told, and the general atmosphere in the country, the deacons all think that that may actually be a bad thing. We'd like for you to be the troop leader instead of Tucker."

When Tig continued to stare blankly at him, the preacher realized what was going on.

Tig had no idea about his twin brother.

The preacher tried a different approach, thinking it may be a softer blow if it wasn't direct, but sort of sideways.

"Tig? Ever wonder why Tucker's not married?"

Tig hadn't wondered. Tucker was just...Tucker. He'd always done things in his own way and in his own time. No one in the family worried about that.

The preacher tried again.

"Don't it seem strange that Tucker and Jon have been roommates for so long? They've been sharing that house together for over ten years."

Tig had never really thought about it. With his life so full and busy- wife, kids, more kids, work, church, it left very little time for him to pay much attention to what Tucker was doing- as long as he seemed happy and didn't ask him for money, that was good enough.

The preacher would have to be much more direct.

"Tig. Tucker and Jon's house is a two bedroom house and they use one bedroom for their African Violet collection."

Tig stared straight ahead of him at the preacher's desk. There was a statue on the desk of Santa Claus kneeling at the manger. Tig had always loved that statue, but now it would remind him of the moment he found out his twin brother was gay.

"Tucker ain't gay!" Tig heard his own voice without realizing he was talking.

The preacher looked at him sadly.

And Tig was in his truck and driving to Tucker and Jon's house- he'd straighten this right out and go back to set that preacher straight.

He pulled into the driveway and cut off the engine, staring at the house as though he'd never seen it before.

Even though it was deep in the woods, it was surrounded by a swath of deep green lush lawn, weedless and perfect. There were shrubberies and perennial flowers dotted here and there, serving as backdrops for the gnomes.

The gnomes and the bird baths were reflected in the mirrored garden globes.

Holy crap. Tucker was gay.

Impossible.

As in a trance, Tig got out of his truck and walked past Tucker's Camry and Jon's Civic. He paused to knock once on the brightly-painted front door and then walked in.

His twin brother and Jon were in the kitchen, making sandwiches. Both were wearing jeans and flannel shirts and it was clear they'd been out working in the yard. Each of them had a freshly opened beer on the counter.

"Hey, Tig- want some lunch?" Tucker smiled at him, but the smile faded when he saw Tig's face.

"God, Tig- what's wrong? Someone die? You look like shit!" Tucker came around the counter with a beer and handed it to Tig.

"Tucker? You gay?"

Tucker started to laugh, and then realized Tig was dead serious. Jon said, "I'll be outside if you need anything" and headed out the back door, grabbing an extra beer along with his open one and his sandwich.

"Tig? Have a seat. I guess we need to talk."

"I ain't sitting down, Tuck. Just answer the damn question."

Tucker looked at his brother and it was like looking in a mirror. They were identical twins and had always been impossible for people to tell apart- even their momma had had to dress them in different colors as babies or she'd get 'em mixed up.

 As toddlers, they'd quickly learned the hilarity of purposely deceiving people regarding their identity, they'd regularly warted their teachers and friends all through school, and even now it was difficult for people to tell one from the other.

They walked alike, talked alike, had the same gestures and quirks…they were identical in all ways.

Or so Tig had thought.

"Tuck?"

Tucker looked at his brother- at the confused pain in his eyes. He'd rather cut off his own arm than say or do anything to hurt him, but there was no way to avoid this.

He should've told him years ago.

But the time never seemed right- they were just kids when Tucker realized that he had no interest in girls. When all the other boys were collecting girlfriends like trophies, Tucker concentrated on his school work and the boy scouts. He'd made Eagle Scout with flying colors.

Then he'd progressed to being scout leader and he knew he'd never be able to do that if he 'officially came out'.

People just didn't understand that 'gay' does not equal 'pedophile'. They just didn't. Once you came out as gay, there was a large portion of the population, especially in these parts, who would

196

then never trust you with a little boy, or little girl (?) or even their dog.

So years had turned into decades and he'd never told anyone in his family.

He'd met Jon and they'd moved in together. Neither one fit the profile of 'typical gay man' whatever the hell that was supposed to be.

They both worked in construction, both wore jeans and work boots, both had the tanned and muscled bodies of a working man.

They drank beer and shot pool.

"Tuck? Tell me it ain't so."

Tucker sighed and shook his head. "I'm sorry, Tig."

All the blood drained out of Tig's face and his hands balled up into fists. "What the *hell*, Tuck? How could you *do* this to me? We're more than brothers! We're *twins* for fuck's sake!" He pounded on the kitchen counter so hard Tucker was afraid he'd break his own hands.

"Tig, please calm down! It's not like I did it on purpose! I wanted to tell you, but I was afraid of…this."

Tig was unable to listen, beyond reasoning, merely talking out loud.

"You're my kids' godfather! You spend all that time with the boy scouts! What the hell have you done to those kids?"

Now it was Tucker's turn to be angry.

"Tig- I'm me. I'm the same person you thought I was- I'm a hard-working, moral man who goes to church and loves his family and friends. I have a home and a mortgage and shop for groceries. I cook dinner and live with the person I love, just like you do. Why would I hurt a child? I love those kids! Just because I'm gay doesn't mean I'm a child molester- you do know there's a difference, right? Please tell me you know that. Please."

Tig looked right through Tucker. "I don't know shit anymore, Tuck. Just…stay away from me. Stay away from my kids and stay away from the church and the scouts. Preacher's right- the world's doomed unless we start standing up for what's right and this ain't it."

"Tig!" But he was out the door, in his truck and gunning the engine. In less than thirty seconds all that was left was the cloud of dust his truck left and the sound of Jon's weed trimmer in the back yard.

Tig just drove.

He couldn't go back to see the preacher.

He couldn't go home.

He decided to stop at the liquor store and then go out to the Range- no one would be there now. This required some serious thinking, and nothing was more conducive to thought than beer and solitude.

He parked his truck in his usual spot under the shade of the biggest sweet gum tree and exactly halfway between the shooting bench and the outhouse.

The big diesel truck sputtered, coughed and was silent.

Taking a long pull of the first beer, Tig closed his eyes and leaned back in his seat, trying to make some sense of the last few hours.

All he could think of was Tucker.

He and Tucker as kids, doing all the regular kid stuff- knocking each other around, building forts and tree houses, learning to shoot, camping out in their back yard. They'd really never been apart.

What the hell had happened?

When the hell had it happened?

They'd remained close in high school even though Tig had started chasing the girls and Tucker…hadn't. Tig was so busy with his own hormones that he never thought about what might be going on with Tucker. Could he have done anything to stop it?

He didn't think so. He didn't *want* to think so because that would implicate him in his brother's sin.

His brother's sin.

Tucker and Jon. Jesus.

Now he couldn't get *that* out of his head.

How could he have known? They were regular guys. They weren't swishy; they didn't show any untoward affection between them…at least in public.

But he should've known. He was Tucker's brother. His twin.

And apparently he was the only one who *didn't* know. He cracked open another beer. Did his parents know? His other brothers?

He didn't think so. No, he was sure of it.

They didn't know.

But the preacher did.

The preacher.

The preacher had stood up before God and everyone and said that this country was going to Hell in a hand basket because of the Gays.

God was angry with America for her acceptance of the Gays.

It was on all the news on TV- America needed to be cleansed and then God would love her again.

Tucker was his brother.

Tucker.

Tucker and Tig.

Tucker and Jon.

The third beer opened with a *snap* and a hiss.

Tig caught something from the corner of his eye and he turned to his left.

Almost blending in with the fallen leaves and foliage, a Copperhead was winding its way across the open lawn of the Range and Tig had the unbidden thought that he was in Eden.

The tall trees whispered in the breeze and the sun warmed his face. Birds were singing and crickets were chirping and everything was damn near perfect...

...except for that damn snake.

Tig took his Ruger Mark III out of the glove box and walked towards the retreating serpent.

It boasted the perfect combination of proven design and reliability. With a rigid barrel/receiver connection, automatic bolt-hold-open latch, comfortable, rugged steel grip frame, contoured ejection port, easy-to-grasp tapered bolt ears, and rigidly mounted sights for consistent accuracy, this was the little handgun he kept loaded with birdshot to deter stray dogs on the farm...or dispense with pesky snakes.

He closed in on the Copperhead and it sensed him there. It paused and turned its head slightly, inquisitively.

Its eyes were unblinking and non-committal and it started off again just a little faster than before. Not that it was afraid of Tig, but he had been sized up and dismissed as of no use.

The first shot was to the body and the snake whipped around convulsively.

The second shot was to the head, and obliterated the snake's eyes, nose and most of its forehead, effectively killing it.

It's a strange thing- the behavior of a natural being to unnatural circumstances.

Though clearly dead due to lacking most if its head, the body continued to move in a creepily casual manner.

The third shot was point-blank to the remains of the head and the body finally surrendered to the sad acceptance that it wasn't going anywhere anymore.

Tig got the shovel he always kept in the bed of his truck and scooped up the body of the Copperhead, carrying it into the woods and tossing it as far as he could away from the Range.

Nothing eats a dead snake, and they stink to high heaven.

Tossing the shovel back into his truck, Tig got back in and opened the fourth beer, then turned the key in the ignition.

Pausing to look around, he felt nothing but love for the woods and the Range- this was his Home and this was worth fighting for. The snake didn't have a choice about being a snake, but it was evil in Eden and it was evil here.

Tig had thought it all through and it all made perfect sense now. He was suddenly calm as calm could be. He understood what needed to be done.

The little Ruger had done its job against the serpent in Eden, but what Tig needed now was locked in the box in the backseat of his truck. Because he never left home without it.

His BAR LongTrac Stalker, just like the one Tag now had. He chuckled to himself about that. Tag had had a hard on for one like this for years and it *had* been fun to whip it out and parade around in front of him with it.

Sure it had been sort of a dick move, but that's what brothers did to each other, didn't they?

Brothers.

Tig shoved that word to the back of his head in disgust. Dangling your superior tool of destruction under your brother's nose was one thing.

Turning yourself gay and not caring about what that did to your brother, your twin, your family and your country?

That was sinful. And selfish. And sick.

Tig's heart was breaking as he tossed the fifth empty can through the back window and it clanked and rolled around the bed of the truck, bouncing off of the shovel and the locked gun box.

How could Tucker have betrayed him so?

Being heartbroken pissed him off and being pissed off gave him focus and purpose, but he knew he needed a clear head for this and he tucked the last full beer into the backseat cup holder.

He'd save that one for afterwards.

Tig Carroll, 34 years old, Christian, American, Heterosexual Married Father of Christian American Heterosexual children, turned onto the blacktop road and headed back to his brother Tucker's house.

He was on a mission from God to save the world as he knew it, and by God nothing was going to stop him.

<u>Epilogue</u>

Fate strolled through the woods, admiring the beauty of it. It really *was* just like Eden.

Something people don't realize is that the beauty of the wilderness comes not from a lack of danger, but an overabundance of it.

Mother Nature is not tender-hearted, nor is She wicked. Life ebbs and flows without regard for any individual.

As she approached the big pine, she hummed softly, and the angry buzzing around the base of the tree quieted and subsided as the swarm abandoned Tig's unmoving body and marched back underground.

"They always make that one last mistake", she thought to herself.

Setting up his perfect shot, he'd double-checked everything- angle, range, lighting, wind…everything but whether or not he may be inadvertently standing on the near-invisible entrance to a hive of ground bees.

His shot had gone wild, of course. No matter how well-trained, no one stays steady when suddenly covered in pissed-off bees.

Fate bent over, gently closing the eyes that stared straight ahead in amazement. She traced a line from his nose down his chin, resting for a moment on his chest but knowing there would be no heartbeat.

"Poor Tig. As Ms. Libby would say- "Lordy, you sure stepped in it this time, didn'tcha?"

Sighing, she turned and walked away, a halo of bees softly humming around her head.

BOOK FIVE-

THE WEAKER SEX

<u>Prologue</u>

And the struggle was a mighty one in homes all over this great nation.

Pushed to the brink of their knowledge and resources, it took everything they had to remain calm and focused.

What they were forced to do was so out of character, so unnatural, so unthinkable that it was only their own hunger and that of their crying and pitiful children that they even attempted it at all.

God would see them through this.

What was happening now would truly result in the final perfection of this great nation. The struggle had been long and hard, the sacrifices huge and terrible, but it hadn't been enough.

This would do it. This final act of contrition and obedience would be the gesture that pushed America back into God's good graces once and for all.

If only they could survive it.

God would see them through this.

In homes and apartments, farms and condos all over the country the men pulled themselves up and faced their children calmly and sternly- befitting their role as king of their households and leaders of their families.

Silently they wished that the teenaged girls hadn't been taken as well as the women- this would be so much easier. But they understood.

The only way to guarantee full-scale and complete change was to include all the females of thinking and reasoning age into the total immersion.

Because that shit just had to stop.

God would see them through this.

Just for a moment they saw their wives and daughters in their minds' eyes, waving and smiling as they drove off and they wondered if they'd done the right thing…and they pushed those doubts aside.

Desperate times call for desperate measures.

God would see them through this.

All they needed to do was get through this one weekend without their women and then everything would be better than OK- the final sacrifice would be made, God would smile on this great nation once more, and life would never be the same again...but in the best of all possible ways, according to the government and their preachers.

So they manned up and braved the kitchens and laundry rooms- enemy territory that was completely foreign to them.

Their children were highly skeptical but didn't say anything- children should be seen and not heard and this generation would be raised accordingly. No one was sparing the rod anymore.

No more of that squishy liberal lovey dovey soft-parenting bullshit.

Children need to know their place in life, especially the females.

It was the way God intended- the natural order of the universe.

Men ruled and women submitted. The society had worked beautifully and God had smiled on the nation until the godless liberals had insidiously infected the heads of the women with the notions of free choice, independence, and equality. It'd all gone to hell in a hand basket since then.

After this three day weekend's national conference, that shit would be over for good.

Life would never be the same.

They envisioned the 51 luxury hotels that were hosting the conferences- one in each state and one even in DC itself. This morning they would be bustling with women...*their* women and daughters, mothers and sisters- laughing and talking and thinking they were there for merely female Christian fellowship.

Once more they thought of those women and girls they loved- all godly but flawed. Some too spirited, some too opinionated, but that made them who they were...didn't it?

It didn't matter. This was for the good of the nation and it would be OK. Different, but OK.

The hungry cries of the children became louder and the men shook their heads clear and turned to the task of feeding offspring.

Dawn broke over the 51 luxury hotels and sunlight streamed in through walls of windows, glinting off of polished stainless steel coffee pots and reflecting onto hundreds of donuts and muffins.

Round tables that seated a dozen people each were set with white cloths, red folded napkins and ivory china plates. Crystal vases each containing three yellow carnations, baby's breath and a single fern were in the center of each table, nodding silent welcome to the gentle Christian women who would never be there.

The Camel's Nose

Fate was exhausted. She had dropped fully clothed onto her bed and the events of the last six months swirled around her head in no particular order- a cacophony of idiocy.

She wiggled her scarlet-polished toes and stretched her hands up to meet the gnarled headboard of the old bedstead, gently tracing the whorls by heart.

Burrowing down into the quilt, she closed her eyes and tried to calm her thoughts by bringing up the image of her mother.

Rolling onto her side, she opened up the side table drawer and took out the three photographs she always had with her.

The first two had been familiar to her since she was barely old enough to speak- the photo of her mother and father on their wedding day and the photo of her mother holding a newborn Fate and smiling into the camera with love and adoration for the cameraman- her father.

And then there was the photo she had never seen till after her mother's death.

Filled with shadows and blurred with under-exposure, the full moon was the only illumination, rendering the image shades of black and white even though it had been taken with color film.

It was of the woods behind their house- the same woods that the bullet that had killed her had careened through, and the soft image seemed ethereal and visceral in its feminine power, naked save the gossamer cloak, bare feet not touching the ground, her mother's hair flowed behind her- golden waves in a velvet night.

The first two told her where she had come from and gave her roots. The last one told her who she was and gave her wings.

She had never known her father- he'd died when she was only a month old. Her mother had had many powers and strengths but the ability to conquer cancer was not one of them.

When her father died, a good chunk of her mother's heart had gone with him.

She'd raised Fate with love and devotion but always missed her true soul mate.

There had always been a little voice in Fate's head that whispered that her mother had somehow purposely put herself in harm's way that day.

There were two porches on their old house and the front porch was the sunnier in the afternoons, but for some reason her mom had been sitting on the back porch when the bullet had exited the neighbor's gun- the new one he was trying to figure out with the help of a few beers and his buddies, evaded at least fifty trees of varying sizes and lodged silently and terminally deep in her mother's brain via a small hole in her temple; would've been a sniper's envy.

Fate's mother had always taught her to pay attention to the people around her.

Not in a 'pay attention because everyone is trying to screw you over' way, but in a 'pay attention because everyone is fighting a battle of quiet desperation' sort of way.

Fate looked deep into the photograph of her mother in the moonlight.

It was genetic- as genetic as the brown eyes flecked with green she'd gotten from her father and the wildly luxurious hair in colors of all the precious metals she'd gotten from her mother; the power to see, the power to feel, the power to do.

Her mother's voice echoed in her head. "We can't do everything, but we can always do something.

Everyone on this earth is given gifts. How they choose to use them is what matters."

Fate remembered as far back as she could go and there was always her mother…talking to people everywhere, people she knew but more likely people she didn't know, in all types of surroundings and circumstances. She always did more listening than talking- speaking just often enough to keep the conversation going.

The subject would turn from the mundane things of life- the weather and other small talk- to more personal things. Fate's mother had a quiet strength about her, a confident concern that encouraged everyone to open up to her and convey their fears and needs without even knowing it.

And at the end of the conversation, there was always The Hug.

"Always remember the power of a hug" Fate had heard over and over and over again. "People can tell you what they want you to know with their words, they can reveal their thoughts through their eyes, but only the physical contact of a hug will relay what's truly in their hearts."

Fate, like her mother, could 'feel' another person by touch- a hug told much about someone's energies and intentions. A good hug transferred positive energy from both parties in a warm ebb and flow. If the hug recipient was damaged somehow- hurt or twisted by life and circumstance, the one-way pull of energy sometimes threatened to pull Fate's mother in; into the never-sated hunger of want and need and she had to be careful and brace herself for that contingency.

It was the touching, close and personal, that allowed for a silent and unthinking exchange of information at the most primitive of levels. Fate's mother had only told her about the hugging.

She had no warning for the first time she had sex.

He was a nice boy. He and Fate were in the same social group of kids at school and when the inevitable pairing-off had started, Brian and Fate had just sort of evolved into it.

In the way of teenagers everywhere, most of their sex ed came from each other…the blind leading the visually impaired with confidence that rose above any gaps in their scanty knowledge.

So she and Brian took their turn at bat, moved slowly yet steadily around the bases with pleasure and excitement, and one Friday night at the pasture party after the game, they took off into the woods like all the other young couples, leaving the singles to jeer after them bawdily while toasting them with their ill-gotten beer.

She'd been told that the first time might hurt a little bit and there might be bleeding. To expect some…leakage from the boy's part afterwards but that was okay- if she sat up right afterwards, gravity would let all the sperm fall out.

They undressed each other shyly, able to see their partner's entire body all at once for the first time. No stealthy groping, no nervous glimpses of parts and pieces.

And all in the light of the full moon- how much more romantic could it get?

Fate lay back in the bed of soft pine needles- the blanket she'd brought a barrier between herself and whatever might also be living in the soft natural mattress. She smiled and looked up at Brian.

He was paralyzed for a moment with the wonder of his luck- she was beautiful.

"You okay with this?" he whispered. She nodded, and he lowered himself onto and into her.

When she gasped, he was afraid he'd hurt her and he looked at her in alarm.

"Should I stop?" She shook her head no, but didn't say anything.

She couldn't say anything.

Once he was inside her, she not only felt his physical presence, but she could feel...everything inside him.

Not just an impression of how he was feeling, but his actual thoughts, desires, feelings, memories.

All there in a rush inside her head.

It was powerful.

It was fascinating.

It was terrifying.

She experienced his pain when he'd fallen off his bike at age four and his panic being held down for the stitches he'd needed.

She heard his parents fighting in the night when he was ten, alone in his bed and wondering what would happen to him when they divorced and hating himself for not being able to fix it.

She felt everything he was feeling right now- his flat young torso pushed against her soft breasts, the taste of her mouth on his, her hair tangled gently in his fingers, and the final expulsion inside of her quickly throbbing to a shudder and sigh.

The pain of her tearing hymen was searing and brief, and overshadowed by the visceral tangible fabulous sensations that Brian felt...because as long as they were connected, whatever he felt, she felt.

They lay next to each other, exhausted.

He asked shyly, "Are you okay?" and she nodded silently and mustered a smile before turning away. He spooned up against her and they stayed there for a long while.

She knew one thing without question. She would never venture into intercourse again without protection. She would find a spell to keep herself from being exposed to absolutely everything inside her partner- it was too overwhelming, too frightening, too intimate, too dangerous.

And so she did. For years she refused to have sex without the paralyzing spell she put on her partners- allowing them both to have pleasure without her getting too close, to stay on the surface level.

Under the whispering pines that first night with Brian, she was so distracted by what she'd seen inside of him that she plumb forgot to sit up and let the semen run downhill.

The next day, she told her mom everything and her mom sighed heavily and with regret.

"I'm so sorry- I was foolishly hoping this wouldn't come up yet. Yes, my dear- I will help you. Now and forever."

Together they gathered the Cohosh Black and Blue, Pennyroyal, and Angelica to flush out Fate's uterus just in case, and together they practiced and perfected the spell she'd need to keep herself truly protected, physically and mentally, until she was mature enough, experienced enough, and strong enough to do without it.

She and Brian broke up shortly afterwards.

The teen years are so tumultuous.

<u>The Eye of a Needle</u>

After her mother's death, Fate had drifted- literally and emotionally, trying to figure out both what was worth living for and how she fit into society. All very common problems for a young adult, but for a young adult with what some would call 'powers', even more daunting.

She'd stay a month here, a few months there, never any longer than half a year before moving on to a new town, new society, and new persona.

She didn't want to get too attached to anyone or anything.

Working odd jobs, she was just another human trying to get by- mostly unseen and unnoticed and she tried to help others who were also floating along just underwater...under the surface of the America that thought of itself as grand and noble; never realizing that the only reason they were above water at all was that they were being buoyed by those they couldn't/wouldn't see there beneath their feet. They'd never acknowledge they had any part in the perplexing inability of some segments of society to rise above the surface where they comfortably bobbed along.

Some people are just too lazy and stupid to get ahead in life.

So she did her small part to help those who couldn't help themselves, and as the stranglehold of regressive social policies continued to kill the nation, the politicians inexplicably doubled down over and over again; restricting or eliminating the rights of whole swaths of citizens in the name of god and drunk on the taste of power until even the corporations who'd loosed them as a diversion so they could neatly sew up the government for themselves were alarmed and tried to rein them in.

But it was too late.

The genie was out of the bottle- the Old Testament firmly in the place of the Constitution. The New Testament had been relegated to the back burners where it could be controlled and re-interpreted...because at face value it sounded positively socialist.

The only parts of the New Testament that were still considered relevant were the stories of Jesus' birth (because everyone loves Christmas) and his death and resurrection (because everyone loves Easter)

Also Revelations, because Fire and Brimstone are excellent control devices.

Keep 'em scared straight and in line.

The gun lobby was as strong as ever; stronger in many ways, and people were armed to the teeth and rooted in the Scripture, wary of their neighbors and outright hostile to strangers.

The hammer control was still strictly enforced and the infrastructure continued to decline, but no one cared because it was to keep them safe- rigidly controlled hammers and an abundance of guns would keep them safe.

They were alarmed at first at the deaths and injuries caused by ill-repaired structures, but that was the price of freedom. Wasn't it?

They never spoke about the fact that gun deaths and accidental injuries were wildly out of control, because if you questioned in any way the ready and free access to firearms without limit, you were suspect of being anti-American.

Everyone knew that the only thing that stood between the US citizens and total breakdown of society were the millions and millions of firearms in the hands of...everyone.

The rest of the world finally gave up trying to figure out America's twisted and abnormal love affair with everyone being armed with absolutely no restrictions or training, rhyme or reason, and the US became listed as a third world dangerous place to visit.

They were just jealous because they envied our Freedoms and didn't understand the fundamental importance of an armed citizenry.

Just as soon as the government overstepped their bounds, the armed citizenry would magically form into a cohesive, well-trained militia and Take Back America. The armed citizenry watched and waited in eager readiness.

For all its lauded freedom and equality for all, America was still laughably backwards and segregated.

Like children, people believed if they repeated something often enough and loudly enough, it would morph from fantasy into fact.

America was the Land of Opportunity, unless you were in the disappearing and struggling middle and lower classes, which comprised 99% of the citizens now.

But any day now, all those millions of people at the bottom expected that Lotto ticket to come through…

America had the best health care in the world, if you could afford it. And only the top 1% of people could.

America saw everyone as equals, unless you were a minority. Or female. Or Gay.

And there was the puzzling part.

Even though America had gone back to being a strictly Christian nation and rolled back every unnatural and egregious piece of law to make it so, things were not, in fact, getting better for most people.

They worked longer hours for less pay in more dangerous places because there was no regulation whatsoever.

They sickened and died of ridiculously simple things because they had no access to medications and in many cases, no access to clean water or safe groceries for the same reasons.

Those at the top of the human food chain took more and more, had bought the entire government and were systematically devouring the people below them and the environment they all lived in.

And the armed citizens clutched their guns and looked at others in the same flimsy boat as they were and just knew they were looking at the enemy.

They never considered that maybe the steel-plated warship manned by the corporations and bankers bearing down on them was the real culprit.

Bullheadedly, they took aim and readied to blow holes in the floor of their already tenuous vessels.

Camp CTJ (Come to Jesus) was a pristinely wild yet perfectly square piece of forest overlooking Lake Revenir nestled in the deep woods of the rural South. It attracted church youth groups from several states around not only for the glorious natural testament of God's artistic skills, but for the programs and education promised the campers. Every single camper entrusted to the care of the Rev. Rockford Devine came to the camp for the summer as mere Children of God and left there tanned, fit, clear-eyed Soldiers ready to fight to the death for God and America.

Boys and girls had separate training, of course.

Boys learned the finer arts of shooting, hunting, survival, hand-to-hand combat right along with their daily Bible studies under the stern and sometimes harsh tutelage of Rev. Devine. These were tough times and tough times called for God's young men to be prepared and willing to defend their God and country when required.

Being a Man of God was not for the weak.

Girls were taken under the wing of the Rev. Devine's wife, who was, if possible, even more stern and harsh than her husband. Enid Devine was the physical opposite of her husband.

While Rockford was tall, fit, commanding and muscular in every way with a shock of jet black hair above striking green eyes, Enid was hard-pressed to top five feet, even in heels (which she'd never wear- heels are for whores). Her dishwater blond hair was going prematurely rustily silver and her eyes were permanently tired and never quite sure if they wanted to identify as hazel or gray.

She had that uniquely depressing middle-aged woman body: no longer toned and fit, but not obese- a strange and familiar combination of sturdy and soft that is characteristic of both cookie-baking grandmothers and armed prison matrons.

She took the girls under her wing and into the cage of womanly submission to drill into them their roles in life- mother, wife, helpmeet, property.

The girls were expected to know how to keep house, cook, weather pregnancy and birth in a never-ending succession without complaint or shirking any of their responsibilities. At no time were they to question decisions made by the men in their life- God made men to care for women and children and women to obey men.

Most of the girls fell into this role without complaint or question- a planned life is a secure and safe life. Considering the dangers of the World, this was an appealing place to be.

They'd spend their lives behind and supporting the strong men of God the boys were being trained to be, raising up the next generation of Soldiers for God.

Every once in a while, a girl would come through who questioned her role in life, not content with being sidelined and relegated to second class status.

Enid would see the defiant spark in her eyes and the proud tilt of her chin and know she'd never accept the role of 'helpmeet' without some additional persuasion.

These were sent to the Reverend for further counseling and attitude adjustments.

It didn't take long, normally just a few sessions. Even the very strong were not as big or as strong as Rockford. They'd come back to their own beds the first night outraged, the second night in tears and by the third night limping and sometimes bleeding, sitting gingerly, bruised and torn in places both obvious and unseen. The Reverend would never spare the rod and employed both beatings and rape to put these girls in their place swiftly and surely.

In the end, their eyes were dulled obediently, their heads lowered submissively, and they never questioned their place in life again.

"I started questioning my place in life after my dear mother died. I never knew my daddy and studying my family genealogy seemed the logical thing for me to do." Fate sat demurely across from the Rev. Rockford Devine at a small table for two. The tiny bar and grill was called "Drink Like A Fish" and though neither one of them were drinking, they were enjoying both the warm summer day overlooking the placid lake and the catfish lunch special this little dive was famous for.

She was dressed in a heathery mossy green lightweight summer pantsuit, just elegant enough to be professional and just fitted enough to be sexy.

Her hair ruffled with the breeze, natural metallic hues of gold, silver and bronze forming a soft backdrop for her seriously perfect face- brown eyes flecked with green, straight small nose and full sensuous mouth all unadorned with makeup save a single layer of black mascara.

Her feet crossed primly at her ankles and were encased in simple leather sandals; scarlet toenails peeking out.

The only jewelry she wore was a moonstone ring on the ring finger of her right hand. Her fingernails were short, clean and unpolished.

The scent of Black Orchid drifted directly up out of her barely-visible cleavage and tickled the Reverend's nose enticingly.

Fate had assumed he'd be dressed in the customary black of a preacher, or at least be wearing his clerical collar, and one slender brow had risen approvingly when he had appeared in obviously tailored navy slacks, an expensively casual robin's egg shirt and well-polished shoes.

He did not miss her appraisal of him.

"Well, Miss Devine, I can certainly understand your curiosity regarding your heritage- we all need to know our roots and our place don't we? A need to know that we somehow fit into the Big Picture of things and all." Rockford smiled straight into her eyes in a fatherly and predatory manner.

Fate lowered her eyes obediently momentarily and then raised them up to meet his.

"Reverend, I was so hoping our shared last name would mean that we had blood in common- I understand you do wonderful work at your summer camp near here. That's why I asked to meet with you even though we are unfortunately not kin. I'm just so grateful that Men of Conviction such as yourself are taking a leading role in the training of our young people. These are exciting and blessed times we're living in, aren't they?"

"Why, yes they are- it's a blessing and a privilege to be entrusted to train up these fine young people- the boys so brave and filled with the fire of the Lord and the girls so willing and softly gracious."

Fate listened with her head tilted slightly. "Do you ever find some of the girls less than happy about their chosen roles?"

Pausing for just a moment, the Reverend smiled sincerely, wolfishly. "Every once in a while. It just takes a little patience and persuasion and then they are right as rain."

After lunch was over, he gave Fate a tour of the camp.

It was a week between sessions and Enid had gone over to the next big town to shop up at the Walmart and spend the night with her sister and family.

The camp was completely deserted.

Sunset on the dock was perfection and Rockford offered Fate a cup of tea before she drove back to the city for the night.

Of course they didn't mean for it to happen...good God-fearing folks never do because that would be sinning.

One thing led to another and they were naked as Adam and Eve in the bed that sat oddly and a little disturbingly in the back corner of his office.

As soon as she entered the cabin, Fate almost passed out from the fear permeating the place. She knew in an instant what the bed was doing in his office- it was for the 'attitude adjustment' of the girls with spirit.

Every cell in her body ached to flee, but she remained outwardly calm and even managed a paper-thin veneer of affectionate flirtation towards this monster acting as an agent of a loving God.

She could waste nothing on fear. It would take everything inside her to do what needed done here.

She lay quietly on the bed, had lain down of her own volition while feeling the multitude of young girls who had been roughly thrown there.

Contact with the bedclothes intensified her connection with every single victim but she managed a sultry 'come hither' smile as the Rev. Rockford Devine rolled smoothly on top of her.

She'd asked him, conversationally over tea, if such harsh treatment was necessary to get the troublesome girls in line and he'd smiled as though talking to a toddler. "Perhaps it seems so, but we need to look at the Big Picture- what we're trying to accomplish here is obedience to our Lord that is adhered to by the entire nation. That's quite a task and you know you have to break a few eggs to make an omelet." He winked and took her hand to lead her to the bed.

The fear that lived in the bed pushed its way up and through her, meeting the pressure of his body on top of hers, and in a single motion, she neatly flipped him onto his back.

His green eyes widened in surprise, but his penis was still comfortably tucked completely inside her and she showed no inclination to remove it, so he smiled amiably. "I'm not normally on the bottom, but for such a lovely lady I'll try anything once."

She returned the smile sweetly. "Good to hear, darlin'. Because I guarandamntee you've never done this before."

He was completely paralyzed.

As she rocked calmly on top of him, rising and falling, in and out in a rhythm as old as humanity, he saw the faces of every young girl he'd raped, felt their pain and fear, over and over again her metallic locks bobbed up and down with the motion of her body, framing her face that had become a flashing slide show of those girls with only one difference from when he had pushed them onto that same bed, yanking their undergarments down and brutally shoving himself into them while they were paralyzed with fear, pain and the strength of him smothering the very soul out of them.

Now their faces showed no fear- it was all on his own.

They laughed and smiled and cheered as he experienced their pain and he couldn't stop what was happening any more than they could.

Just a moment after he swore he couldn't take any more, he inexplicably climaxed in a white hot fire of agony, and he gasped and gurgled and was still.

The obituary would read that the Rev. Rockford Devine expired while asleep in his bed- the victim of sudden pulmonary edema brought on by undiagnosed congestive heart failure.

Fate shrugged and acknowledged that "drowned in his own Evil" was probably too graphic a description for most tender folks.

.

The Camel's Back

Fate couldn't bear to think of the Big Picture as described by the Reverend- she was just one little person, after all. So she did what she could, for those she crossed paths with and tried not to dwell on the rest of them.

It would take a miracle to help them all.

Miracle Monday was the name of the local bible study group in the small church on the other side of Lake Revenir, across from the former Camp CTJ- now closed due to the tragic death of the Reverend.

God always seemed to call the good ones home first.

Fate had secured employment as the church secretary after the widow Enid Devine moved over to the next big town and in with her sister and family.

"No, I'm sorry- I'm no relation to them, but I hear he was a Godly man", she said at least a hundred times those first few weeks.

She needed time to heal and regroup, and this was a calm and non-threatening place, as places went nowadays.

She worked in the church office, typing the weekly services and scheduling the various weddings and funerals, spent evenings quietly in her tidy little rent house secured by one of the deacons, and took in Miracle Mondays with the other women.

It was easy, and low-key and lulling.

She was so completely immersed in the sedating atmosphere she almost missed the tickle that started in the back of her brain, turning into a whisper that was first gentle as a spring mist and then insistent as June bugs.

As accustomed as she was to the voices in her head, this one stood out because it wasn't hers.

All along, in this brave new patriarchy it had been the women who had stood by their men, the way God had intended.

Fate had now been privy to the kitchens and playgrounds, taverns and churches and heard the conversations. They had started out strong and sure, secure in the protection of their men and their Lord…in that order.

"Thank goodness our country has turned back to its Christian roots- now we'll really see America in her greatness again!"

Once hammer control had been implemented, they'd made gentle mention to their menfolk of the sad states of their homes and workplaces and softly inquired about getting them fixed- in effect, questioning the leadership of the nation and by association, their own men's leadership of their families.

They didn't make that mistake again.

When their children sickened and died for lack of health care and clean food and water, they gathered together in groups large and small, praying fervently for favor, and striving in their daily lives to be good enough to be answered, righteous enough to be heeded.

With each tiny body lowered into the ground, the men became more hardened and distant and the women more silent and inwardly frantic.

A few women here and there made quiet suggestions to their proudly-armed and ready-to-take-back-America men that perhaps now...now that there were no decent-paying jobs, or safe workplaces or drinkable water or eatable food or accessible health care and their homes were *still* crumbling around them...just maybe *now* was the time for that rallying-round and taking-back stuff they kept strutting around about.

They didn't make that mistake again.

So the women watched their men become less human and their homes become less habitable and their children die.

They watched their gay sons and daughters- Children of God all- be ostracized and even sacrificed in the name of Saving America and bringing her back around to God's good graces.

They gathered together in groups large and small, praying and studying and reading the Bible- looking for relief and answers and understanding.

They studied the Old Testament and its begats and harshness and law after law.

They learned the Psalms and committed them to heart for the small solace they provided.

They celebrated Christmas and cried over Good Friday and thrilled over Easter.

They read through the Revelation, and were genuinely horrified and cowed by the predictions therein.

But it wasn't enough.

One by one, bible studies all over the country turned quietly and almost secretly to the teachings of their Jesus.

One by one, they attracted women like Fate- with different viewpoints, different strengths, and where there is actual communication and listening and learning, true power is never far behind.

Fate sat in the circle, and the small tickle at the back of her head continued.

Outwardly, she'd been attentive to the opening prayer. Inwardly, she was trying to place the voice. So familiar, she could almost smell the herbs; see jet black hair and ice-blue eyes. And in a flash of memory and recognition there she was- Datura.

"It's about time, Sister! I was starting to think you don't love me anymore." Fate could hear the good-natured pouting from hundreds of miles away.

Because of her shyness regarding her powers, Fate had never really pursued friendships as a child. She tended to keep everyone at arm's length. Even as an adult, she was ever the polite stranger, never the best friend.

Until the day she had been wandering through the unofficial commune of Centerville West, getting a feel for the place and its people.

She'd ordered food from a street vendor and was patiently waiting, when a voice in her head clearly said, "I'd never eat there- they call it 'Kitty's Kart' because that's what she serves- cat meat."

Fate whipped around and almost collided with a woman who was walking past.

"What did you say?"

Ice blue eyes stared into her brown eyes flecked with green. "I'm sorry- I didn't say anything- do I know you?"

Fate wondered to herself if she was hearing things.

"Ahhh…I see now. Yes- you're hearing me. Welcome to Centerville West and happy to meet you" Datura said aloud, extending a hand in friendship.

Fate looked down at her hand suspiciously.

Smiling warmly, Datura thought, "This is your first contact with someone else like you, isn't it?"

And Fate heard her loud and clear, and suddenly she wasn't alone anymore.

It was Datura who taught Fate about the connection between women of power- some called it telepathy; the Christians called it the Devil's work.

This was more than a little hypocritical from people who relied heavily on Faith and Miracles.

Everything on Earth is connected; some things obviously, and some under the surface. Everyone on Earth is connected; sometimes obviously, and sometimes...not.

Sitting in the small church bible study, Fate looked for all the world like she was concentrating mightily on today's lesson- like all of their lessons they incorporated much of the Old Testament patriarchal attitudes imploring and demanding that the women strive for their highest goal- to be obedient unto their men, and by association, to God.

While she was connected to the women in the room with her by virtue of birth and gender, she was communicating in a recently-formed mental web with other women all over the nation- all in their own little church groups and all seeing where this grand new America would end up: the goal was to make women second class citizens...again.

Hell, if they thought they could get away with it, women would be listed as property…again.

Well, they'd be damned if they'd go down without a fight. A chuckle murmured softly in all their heads as they realized as far as the menfolk went, they were already damned.

So what the hell, right? May as well raise a fuss while going down.

Gently, carefully, quietly, kindly, the women with powers much older than this whipper-snapper of a nation turned the thoughts of their own little groups away from their men and what they were being told to believe and do, and back into what they all knew and saw was really happening.

Is this what they wanted for themselves? No access to health care, no voting rights, no say in anything that concerned them?

It didn't matter so much- they had all been raised to obey and support everyone else around them.

Is this what they wanted for their friends and communities? No social services, whole segments of society judged and condemned to be eternally 'less than'- old people, minorities, gays, women…them?

And the women paused in thought, then assured and reassured each other that if things got too bad, their armed men would do something. They had promised them they would.

Fate and those like her knew they couldn't push too hard or they'd push the others away; an unknown future is always more scary than a known present even if the present is awful. The breaking point must be reached.

What they had to do was quietly turn the tide in a manner that caused a unified swell of channeled positive change instead of a wildly unpredictable and violent tidal wave that would only make things worse for the nation, and for these individual women.

Bit by bit, little by little, they helped the others see that things already *were* too bad, already had gone too far, and that their men were not going to do a thing about it. Ever.

And they focused more and more on the teachings of Jesus and less and less on the Old Testament.

Love thy neighbor as thyself.

Judge not lest you be judged.

The meek shall inherit the Earth.

Jesus treated the women around him with respect and as equals.

The contrast between the actual teachings of the Son of God and what they had been taught was the godly way to live was stark and horrible and completely at odds with each other.

When the time was right, they asked their final and deciding question.

"Is this what you want for your daughters?"

The unanimous response was a visceral and overwhelming, "NO!"

And so the Gentle Reunion for the Awareness of Christian Evangelical women was born- GRACE for short.

Publicly, this would be the largest gathering of women in the history of the USA. The capitol city of every state and the District of Colombia would host their own- it was going to be *that* big dwarfing every other revival anywhere. There would be speakers and conferences but over and above all else, there would be intensive and exhausting training in the womanly arts...because there were still a few holdouts to the sinful old ways- women who still thought they had the right to their own property, opinions, thoughts over and above the men in their lives.

It was very annoying and counter-productive to the America they were all longing for.

This weekend would squelch that once and for all, and America would finally have been taken back...all the way back to a day where men said, "Jump" and their women implored, "How high?" the gays and the brown people would be relegated to the back of the bus once again, the bankers and businessmen could blast full-speed ahead with their version of 'economic recovery and growth', and openly-armed white men would rule...everything.

Awesome.

Finally.

Hallelujah!

"Ready?" Datura's voice was strong and clear in Fate's head and the heads of 49 others just like them around the nation.

Fate looked at the women in front of her- they'd grown so strong in the last few months, so determined and sure of themselves while keeping up their accepted roles in public and at home.

"Ready?" she asked them aloud.

Every one of them raised their right wrist- adorned with a WWJD bracelet.

What *would* Jesus do? He'd do what he always did- protect the weak, feed the hungry, love his neighbor and chase the money-changers out of the temple.

Time to Take Back America.

"Let's rock and roll," Fate said aloud, and in every state of the nation, the women went home to instruct their menfolk on the care and feeding of offspring, make sure everyone would have enough clean underwear and socks for the weekend, and pack for the conference.

Epilogue

Dawn broke over the 50 State Capitols and the White House and sunlight streamed down and was absorbed, sucked into the black robes and hoods of the silent ring of figures encircling each building- a dark halo of determination dozens of figures deep all the way around.

The hastily-rallied law enforcement surveyed them with suspicion and more than a little nervousness.

They were accustomed to being the ones in black- the ones with no faces.

There was no clue as to whether or not the figures were armed and no one knew exactly why they were there.

At 7am, the news media received the following message and it was broadcast on the TV, the radio, the internet all at once.

"We are America, and we have had enough.

We waited for the government to help the citizens when the corporations took control of the nation's resources both natural and economic.

We waited for the preachers to stand up for the suffering people- out of work, homeless, penniless, hungry, and sick.

We waited for the proud and armed citizenry to protect the weak and the oppressed and right the above wrongs.

We wait no longer.

We are America's women, and we are done waiting.

We are your mothers, your sisters, your grandmothers and wives. We are all here- we stand right in front of you.

Turn the nation over to us or fire on us. Follow your hearts as we follow ours.

Either way, we have had enough."

After a brief nationwide tele-conference, the general and expert opinion was that the women were not armed and the order was given to advance on the figures and take them into custody- using force only as a last resort, but absolutely using force if necessary.

At 7:15am the officers started to move towards the still-silent figures and in one fluid motion, the figures removed their hoods.

The ranks paused momentarily and then continued forward until here and there came a shout-

"*Stop*! That *is* my mom!"

"Hold up! That's my sister!"

"Holy shit! *Granny*???"

Sensing indecision, the commanders urged them on, stating emphatically that the goal was not to hurt anyone; just to put a stop to this folly and send them all home after a mildly humiliating strip search at the police station and a few hours in jail to teach them a lesson.

At 7:30 the women all casually brushed aside their black robes, revealing holsters and handguns, but not touching them or looking at them; just staring impassively and silently at the approaching line of lawmen dressed in riot gear.

The police did more than halt- they stopped in mid-step and backed up instinctively, their confusion and indecisiveness was palpable and crystalized as a worried murmur throughout their ranks.

In every headphone and earpiece there was an instant and almost gleeful command. "We have armed opponents- I repeat- they are armed. Engage with force immediately!"

Softly at first, then growing louder but never any louder than a soothing speaking voice, the women spoke as one.

"I am an American- I am your mother. I am an American- I am your daughter. I am an American- I am your grandmother. I am an American- I am your wife. We are American citizens- we have stood always with our country and with you. Who are you and where do you stand?"

They had known, these women standing in defiance of everything their society demanded of them, that there would be a few in every crowd.

A few of the men tasked with disbursing them would be...damaged somehow and would absolutely and without pause pull the trigger on even their own mother when directed.

And in the silence that followed their proclamation, it happened in all 51 places where black-robed women met black-garbed military and police.

Several shots were fired and several women fell, the crumpled black fabric blooming deeper ebony with the addition of their scarlet blood.

Just as quickly, the shooters were knocked down and disarmed by their own ranks- still not sure how to handle this, but knowing that killing these women was not what they signed up for.

The other women never moved; toward their fallen or towards their own guns, they just looked deeply and unwaveringly into the eyes of their opposition- their husbands, sons, neighbors, and friends.

In the mind's eye of every policeman and militia member facing the women in all 50 states and the District of Colombia they saw it clearly and for the first time.

Their female relatives being treated as less than them...not the 'different but equal' the preachers and government told them they were, but less than.

The women who birthed them, raised them, sacrificed for them and now stood before them ready to face death to take back the country from the backwards hell hole it had become.

Firm yet determined, as they had been every day of their lives.

One by one the policemen joined the ranks of the women and they advanced on the capitol buildings and the White House together, leaving the headphones and ear pieces screaming impotently into uninterested blades of grass.

BOOK SIX-
HELL HATH NO FURY

Prologue

"No good deed goes unpunished."

Fate heard Datura's voice as clearly as if she had been standing right next to her.

But of course, that was impossible. Datura was dead. Fate had not heard the shot- she was several hundred miles away at the time. But she knew the instant it happened because over everything else that was going on she heard Datura's voice in her head.

"Shit. I always miss the happy ending."

And then nothing.

She'd fallen silently, raven hair flowing out of the hood of the black robe as her crimson blood flowed from the center of her chest.

One of 153 women who lost their lives on the day they took America back. Of course they themselves never fired a shot. That was never their intent.

The loss of 153 was bad enough; if they'd tried to win in a gun battle with the US police and military, they would've been slaughtered outright, it would've made a momentary blip on the media, and the tide wouldn't have turned away from the disastrous regressive black hole it had been funneling into seemingly faster and faster in a sickeningly dizzying death-spiral.

But they'd done it.

Wrested away the government from the bankers and corporations, cleared the Senate, House and White House of the batshit-crazy bible-pounding Tea Party and corporate lap-dogs, and gotten things back on track.

Relatively bloodless, but not clean.

This sort of thing never was.

There had been change-of-guard pains, growing pains, the pain and anger of loss on the part of the recently-in-power and the pain of not knowing exactly where to go from here on the part of the newly elected representatives, who had been elected in a brand new manner - no expensive campaigns; people who were not slick career politicians or businessmen with ulterior motives were nominated by people who actually knew them.

All donations came strictly from individuals, each individual was limited to giving $1,000 and every cent was used for actually doing something for the local community that was related to the nominee's platform and passions. Healthcare, education, women's or minority issues, infrastructure- all slated and used for real things- community clinic supplies, school books, road and bridge repair, small business start-up loans.

The media then covered the progress and completion of all the above with the candidate squarely in the center of the press.

Publicity, proof of commitment and shit actually getting done no matter who won the election- win/win/win.

Corporations were given a choice- they could operate with no tax loopholes, no offshore accounts and no outsourcing of anything from customer service to manufacturing, they had to pay living wages and provide safe working conditions and the workers had to have ownership of the company.

Or they could leave.

Banks were broken up, leaving local banks and credit unions doing business with the 'old-fashioned hometown' attitude and responsibility that keeps a financial institution healthy and honest.

Hammer Control was repealed absolutely and the country was quickly being repaired and restored.

Those who had hoarded huge stockpiles of guns and ammo were sure this would be the End of the World As They Knew It; "For damn sure this ain't the America I want to live in!" and demanded to be allowed to secede from the rest of the nation.

~~Permission was granted~~ they won the hard-fought battle for their independence, and the Free State of Wyoming was formed and surrounded by the longest, highest razor wire and electric fence possible, at the new residents' request.

Some of their family members went with them, but most declined- stating they'd 'take their chances' here in the 'ruins of America'.

So, overall, things were going pretty well- certainly much better than they had been headed before.

Of course, humans being the twitchy and disagreeable creatures they are, there were bits and pieces of unpleasantness here and there.

Fate found herself smack in the center of one such scenario, and had maintained a pretty good outlook about it all until she heard her dead friend's voice in her head.

"No good deed goes unpunished."

And she knew she was probably in deep shit.

Shit Happens

Fate sighed deeply and shook her head at the all-too-familiar scenario being played out in front of her.

On the one hand, she didn't know what those who were now in a precarious position had expected. On the other hand, she wasn't sure how these current actions were being justified by the people committing them.

In the wake of the ousting of those who'd decided "We the People" applied only to those who were white, and rich, and mostly male, their loyal and ardent followers found themselves literally abandoned and under attack.

It came as a horrible shock when their leaders turned their backs on them the second it had become clear that this country was no longer theirs for the pillaging.

With the far right fundamental death grip suddenly loosened, the entire country had taken an enormous lung-filling breath of fresh air and relief and then exhaled all their frustration and anger back onto the minions and henchmen who'd persecuted them for so long- minions and henchmen who looked like their neighbors, employers, acquaintances, co-workers.

It was the epitome of irony that for years the fundamental Christians had been wailing and gnashing their teeth about being persecuted, when what was really happening is that while they had as much freedom as anyone else, they were not granted special status.

They wailed when they were asked to take the Nativity Scene off of the courthouse lawn…and carry it across the street to the church yard.

They gnashed their teeth when told they could not start every public school day with a Christian prayer over the intercom…but there would be a moment of silence so every student could talk to their own god…or not.

They just about had an apoplexy when the public school teachers insisted on teaching evolution in…science class, instead of the creation story.

All these horrible indignities that had so sorely infringed upon their God Given Rights, all had been blessedly avenged when the Tea Party government had taken hold of the nation and now?

Over.

It was all over.

They were heartbroken.

They were confused.

They were pissed.

They knew in their hearts that if they'd managed to take over America once, they could do it again!

The problem was that once they weren't in power any more, all those people *they* had so mercilessly persecuted in the name of their God were still here.

Yessiree, Bob. All the Liberals, Progressives, Blacks, Mexicans, Gays and Women were all still here.

And they were unaccountably not willing to forgive, forget, get over it and let bygones be bygones, "No hard feelings, ya'll".

Go figure.

Fate was striding towards the crowd as all this played in her mind and without pausing she stepped cleanly between the two groups of people gathered in the restaurant parking lot and turned to face the angry ones.

"Just what do you think you're doing?" she asked the obvious leader- a surprisingly tiny woman of Hispanic heritage named Maria.

Maria looked at the people huddled up behind Fate with disgust. "I don't have to let them into my restaurant- we don't need any of their kind stinking up the place."

Someone tapped Fate on the shoulder and she turned to look into the most intense amber eyes she'd ever seen. With some difficulty, she lowered her eyes to what was being shown her- a hand printed sign that had been taped to the door of the establishment-

No Bibles

No Praying

No Tea Party Whites Allowed

Fate considered the people who were being so shunned. They had clearly just come from church, all in their best Sunday garb. The woman with amber eyes was wearing the ubiquitous long-skirted jumper and white blouse that seemed to define the fundamental church ladies. Her hair was trying to behave, but insisted on wisping away on its own here and there- little sprays of independence in shades of brunette.

Her face showed mild confusion and consternation, and an innate kindness. Fate's eyes met hers again and they smiled at each other warmly.

"This ain't right! We've been coming to Maria's after church for years and we ain't going to be turned away now! Gracie? Let's go." And the woman was yanked away by a tall man in black jeans and a white starched shirt. His bolo tie was clasped with a chunk of turquoise and the black leather matched his boots.

Gracie had no choice but to follow and did so silently. Fate gasped quietly and rubbed her arm.

She looked down and there were four finger-shaped bruises appearing on her upper arm right where the man had grabbed Gracie. She rotated her arm and saw the thumb mark on the other side.

Quickly, she stepped in front of the man and said, "Perhaps you just need to find another place to eat...somewhere you'd be welcomed."

The man glared at Fate, and Gracie soothingly interjected. "You know, she's got a point, Duncan.

There's Sugar Pie's Café right over yonder- they've got a right good Sunday buffet."

There were murmurs of agreement from the rest of the group, who were clearly uncomfortable thinking about eating lunch in a place they weren't welcomed.

Who knew what the cooks and servers might do to (or in) their food?

Sugar Pie's may deep fry everything on the menu in peanut oil but at least the owners and staff were like themselves- not disgruntled (most likely illegal) Mexicans.

As the church-goers made their way down the street and the loaded buffet of chicken fried steak, fried okra, onion rings and lard-crusted pie all washed down with tea so sweet it makes your teeth holler, Fate turned her attention to Maria and her staff.

"Really? Discrimination? How on Earth is that going to help anything?"

Maria's dark eyes flashed and she didn't back down, tipping her head up to stare Fate in the eyes unwaveringly.

"Too bad for them. Good to have a taste of their own medicine. How many times was my family told, 'You can't come in here', 'You can't vote here, 'You can't, can't, can't unless you're mowing the lawn or cooking us enchiladas or cleaning our toilets'? We're sick of dealing with them, sick of hearing them, sick of seeing them."

The scent of cilantro and onion, hot flour tortillas and grilled chicken wafted through the doorway and Maria smiled and asked, "You hungry? Come on in- my treat."

Over lunch, the women discussed the snags society was running into on its way to a new way of being defined.

"It's so hard not to push back. We were all pushed up against that wall for so long- especially if you're unfortunate enough to be multiple 'sinners'- female and non-white is bad enough, throw 'gay' into the mix and you've been a special kind of persecuted. The Holy Trinity of the Damned, I call it," and Maria winked at Fate.

Fate laughed. "How *is* Celeste? Apparently not doing very well at keeping you out of trouble."

Smiling with obvious devotion, Maria said, "Ohhh, she's fine- very busy running the women's clinic now that it's been opened again. So many women need so much care, and now they can get it, thank Goddess! How about you? No one has snatched you up out of your endless purgatory in spinsterhood, I see."

Fate gave her friend a distinctly vague look. "Hmmm…guess I just haven't run across the right guy yet."

"Uh huh. You mean 'the right person', Chicka. I saw how you and that Gracie looked at each other."

"Pffft. I like men. I *love* men. Sometimes I think I'm just too…much for most men, though. And I don't mean that in an egotistical way. Just the way it is."

Maria put her hand on Fate's wrist and gently turned her arm to and fro, the bruises almost glowing in the soft light of the restaurant. Her words seemed to hover in mid-air before burrowing themselves into Fate's heart.

"You connect and fall in love with a person's soul, my dear- not their plumbing."

Deep Shit

Children's laughter echoed through the house, music to Gracie's ears as she folded laundry she'd just retrieved from the line and she shook her head and smiled at the liveliness of her brood.

It had been just another normal day- children up, fed, and schooled. Laundry washed and hung. Lunch made, all of them sent to their room to take an afternoon nap or at least a 'just rest your eyes' and now laundry in before making dinner.

Twenty six years old, Gracie had been married at 18 to Duncan. Her father had chosen him for her when she was 16, after Duncan had gone to her father after church one day and stated his intentions.

At her wedding reception Gracie danced with Duncan and that was the second time in her life she'd danced with anyone- the first time was at the Purity Ball her father and she had attended when she was 12.

It was a beautiful affair- she'd been caught up in the magic and the prettiness, the princess-like picture of herself in the mirror and her father so tall, strong and handsome in his suit. Why wouldn't she want him to protect her and choose her husband?

When her father told her she would be married to Duncan, she was secretly relieved. Duncan was a good looking young man from a decent family- she'd known him all her life along with all the other young men in her church.

From the time they were pre-teens, all the girls had wondered who they would marry; sneaking shy peeks at the young men growing up around them. Gracie had been terrified that it would've been someone less easy on the eyes or perhaps with an unfortunate hygiene problem…and then she'd immediately prayed for forgiveness and reminded herself that whoever her father chose for her would be the best choice- one that he'd make after serious and careful consideration.

Surely that was better than the willy-nilly hormone-driven moths-crashing-into-each-other-under-a-streetlight affairs those outside of the church practiced.

Gracie had shuddered at the thought of being set adrift with all the other teens trying to all find their way to adulthood and adult relationships without supervision or oversight.

Sometimes she wondered whether she shuddered from repulsion or excitement but she didn't let herself dwell on that too much.

She had closely-monitored 'dates' with Duncan for two years and then they married; when he kissed the bride it was the first time either one of them had been kissed.

They were very young and very naïve and entered their marriage bed with a mixture of lust and terror.

Gracie had steeled herself for 'it's going to hurt the first time but that's one of the trials of being a woman' and had been surprised when it didn't really hurt- there was a stretching and sharpness but then…nothing.

The first time was over in a matter of minutes- Duncan had been very excited after groping around under the covers. Starting off shyly, he first touched her breasts softly, then gently squeezed them and ran his hands down her sides.

His fingers traced her slim waist and young hips, pausing on her buttocks before flipping over on top of her and quickly finding what he wanted.

She felt the head of his penis pushing at the opening of her vagina and she gasped as he shoved it inside her.

Breathing heavily onto her neck, his hips slapping against hers, she suddenly realized that it didn't really matter that *she* was there at all; all he really needed and wanted was a vagina…any vagina.

Just then, the static pause of his ejaculation lubricated her insides and the final few thrusts were almost pleasant. Her legs impulsively wrapped around his to hold him inside her because she was feeling a warmth and tingling that she didn't want to lose just yet.

"Hey! What're you doing?" Duncan sounded alarmed. "I'm finished, Gracie- lemme go!"

And he turned onto his side with his back to her and quickly fell asleep.

That was eight years and four children ago and their sex life was virtually unchanged.

Duncan was a good man- a hard worker, solid church-goer and well-respected both in their congregation and in the community at large. Thinking that he should be a more attentive lover seemed so trivial and selfish.

So Gracie didn't think about it much-she was too busy, for one thing. Four kids under the age of seven will do that to you.

The almost-seven year old and the five year old were her students; they home schooled like

273

everyone at their church. A lot of people were home schooling who weren't even 'churchy' because without so much as the most basic funding, the public schools had fallen into a horrible state. Now that the government had changed, word was that the money would again flow into the school systems but that wouldn't change what she and Duncan did- they aimed to raise their children up Godly and you can't do that when Sinners are their teachers.

Gracie hadn't been able to attend the 'conference' that caused the government takeover because she'd been too pregnant with their last child to go anywhere except from her rocking chair to the bathroom to bed…other than her normal housework, cooking and child care of course.

She remained puzzled at the whole thing, and she had overheard Duncan's friends telling him how lucky he was that his wife was still 'under control'.

She wasn't sure what that meant but it didn't sound complimentary.

The other women in the church had come home and just settled back into their former roles of good wives and mothers and never mentioned it again.

The husbands tried to pretend that it had never happened, but it was a tenuous and uneasy time within the Church and all of their homes.

Outside the church was even worse. Every single group that had been oppressed and persecuted during the rise and reign of the Tea Party government was lashing back with a vengeance.

In addition to being denied entrance to restaurants and stores, their children were taunted on the few occasions they strayed out of the safety of their congregational peer group. A few had had rocks thrown at (and hit) them, some had been waylaid and roughed up and one of the men who had had car trouble found no help when he knocked on doors in a minority neighborhood- the blinds had been drawn and angry, "You'd better get outta here before I call the cops!" shouts followed by porch lights flicking off were all the reaction he got.

They were unaccustomed to such treatment and it was frustrating and depressing that there was no peace to be had either inside their homes or without.

All they'd been trying to do- bring God back into America, protect women through governance because women don't have the wherewithal to make good business and health decisions, be sure only American Citizens voted, and supporting the strong in society while not enabling the weak- where was the harm in all that?

It just made sense. Good moral sense and good business sense.

The children had stopped giggling together and fallen into a deep afternoon slumber. The warm breeze ruffled the laundry as she folded it, wafting through the window with the scent of gardenias and roses, warmth and sunshine, and something she didn't recognize- a perfume that was spicy and musky, almost masculine but somehow very feminine.

Curious, she went to the front door, opened it and looked in all directions.

Nothing and no one.

Shrugging, Gracie closed the door quietly and a slip of paper glided off of the welcome mat and lit on the top of her bare foot.

Late afternoon playground-break.

City park 4 pm.

Bench next to the sand box

The clock on the wall chimed 3pm.

She'd have to get a wiggle on to get the kids up and be there on time.

Strange Shit

Everything was the same.

Everything was different.

Gracie went about her days as she always had; she cared for her children, her house and her husband with the same honest devotion as she always had.

She attended church and Bible Study on Sundays and Wednesdays as she always had.

Something about her was stronger now, though: she'd always been calm, but now she was focused, and she'd always been kind, but now she was compassionate.

She was looking at the world through new eyes and it was liberating and peaceful.

She told Duncan that she was doing community service in the evenings and she wasn't lying to him.

Fate had squelched the fire at Maria's Taqueria and Maria had grudgingly taken the sign off of the door, but there were many instances of push-back retaliation.

It seemed that every time a Christian was singled out for humiliation and embarrassment, bullying or

278

actual physical assault, two women stepped between the parties and brought an end to the insanity…at least momentarily.

Fate's authoritative demeanor and Gracie's quiet compassion were a winning combination in these situations and they were more than two women trying to keep the peace; they were an example of two very different sides working together for the common good.

The evenings were worse than other times of day-schoolchildren were on the loose and unsupervised and adults were home from work, on the loose and unsupervised. Both groups festered from the constraints society still set on them.

Change is not instantaneous.

So the kids were after-school sugared-up and the grownups were after-work beer-me'ed and it made for volatile meetings between factions.

From bar fights to playground kerfuffles, Fate reminded one side that they should not strive to turn into what they had hated and Gracie reminded the other that their previous behavior had been less than stellar and Christ-like.

And slowly the tide turned and things seemed to settle down.

Sitting in Fate's small apartment after an evening of peace-making, the women were companionably silent while they drank their tea.

Gracie's eyes were closed with weariness and Fate studied her friend closely. She leaned forward and brushed the stray hair from in front of Gracie's face, smelling the good clean scent of fresh laundry, clean babies and her light floral perfume- her children had all pooled together their little allowances, had Duncan take them up to the Walgreens and bought it for her the previous Mother's Day and it's all she ever wore.

Normally, Wind Song was too cloying, too sickly sweet, but on Gracie it mellowed and tamed into something truly lovely.

Fate's hand rested on Gracie's cheek and Gracie's eyes opened; meeting Fate's calmly. Gracie inhaled the now-familiar scent of Black Orchid that Fate always wore and she turned her head ever so slightly to kiss Fate's fingers.

"I'm sorry- I love you." Fate admitted it out loud for the first time.

Gracie knew she should've been shocked, horrified, insulted, revolted.

"I love you, too".

Everything was the same, yet everything was different.

The soft light from the next room illuminated the old bedstead; soft cotton sheets flecked with sprigs of violets underneath them, the women lay together without embarrassment or timidity.

Unlike any heterosexual relationship, it was like looking in the mirror- reaching out and stroking their own parts in the way that they'd done to themselves since birth; everything was familiar and comfortable and no explanations were needed.

There was no having to interject (tenderly yet jokingly) that nipples are not stereo knobs.

Their fingers and tongues knew what would feel good because they knew it from their own bodies.

They were intertwined from their arms to their ankles and they both reached down to spread their labia and their clitorises touched, tender interior to tender interior. The warmth and electricity caused them to clutch each other even closer- lips to lips, breasts to breasts, toes to toes.

Fate could 'see' her lover's life as she always did, but this time it wasn't alarming or foreign and she welcomed in every memory and sensation, feeling as one with another human for the first time in her life and letting herself get lost in it- freely and willingly without hesitation.

Gracie had the sudden realization that for the first time in her life she mattered. Oh, she mattered to her children because they needed her in the way all offspring need their mother. But she and Fate were doing more than having sex-they were making love, and that was a totally new experience for Gracie.

Through it all, Fate's eyes were locked into hers; her head wasn't turned or buried in her neck with closed eyes- and Gracie knew that Fate loved *her*- not because she was expected to like Duncan was, or needed her like her children. Fate was making love to her specifically because she was more than enough- she was everything.

They were everything to each other.

Shit Out Of Luck

"Jesus, Mary and Joseph!!! Gracie???"

Duncan seemed to take up the entire doorway, blocking out the light, darkening life itself.

Gracie gasped and yanked the flowered sheet over her nakedness and she instinctively positioned herself between Duncan and Fate.

Fate shook out her gorgeously mussed hair and it shimmered in shades of gold, silver and bronze. Calmly she met Duncan's wild eyes. "It's OK, Duncan- Gracie loves you. She loves her children and your God. This was all my fault- not hers. Never hers."

Extricating herself from behind Gracie, Fate got out of bed and crossed the room, retrieved a scarlet satin robe from the closet and wrapped it around herself.

Duncan found his voice. "Well, it sure looked like my wife was a willing participant in all this, this, sick, unnatural bullshit!" and he raised his hand as if to strike Gracie.

"Don't hurt him, Fate!" Gracie's voice echoed in her head even though she hadn't said anything.

Fate was so surprised she didn't even see the blow coming.

She was pretty sure the first contact knocked loose a tooth or two, and it was sufficiently dizzying and distracting that she only vaguely registered Gracie spitting out her own tooth onto the bed, spattering the violet sprays with tiny poppy-colored raindrops.

It took a few minutes for Duncan's rage to subside enough to realize that every time he hit Fate, Gracie screamed.

He paused mid-strike and glanced at his wife.

She was crumpled on the bed and the bruises and welts were rising everywhere on her still-naked body. She whimpered pitifully and he felt sick to his stomach.

Fate was severely beaten, but that had been his intent for leading his good, Godly wife astray. Gracie suffering mirror injuries had not been part of his plan.

He loved his wife.

Confusion replaced rage and Duncan froze in uncertainty and suspicion.

"What the hell is happening? What did you do to my wife?"

Fate had painfully pulled herself to the bed and was cradling Gracie, stroking her blood-soaked hair.

"I did nothing to your wife, you asshole. *You* did this! You did this to *us*!"

Duncan couldn't, wouldn't believe he had harmed his wife. He stood dumbfounded and then his eyes lit with a fire from within.

"You're one o' them witches, aint'cha? Word among the menfolk at church has been that our wimmenfolk never woulda done what they done without outside instigation! Never! We been hearing rumors that it was all started by *witches*!"

Gracie sat up on the bed, more angry than hurt now. "Duncan! You really believe that it would've been impossible for women to just get fed up with the way you men have made a mess of things? You never listened to us! You passed laws that made us less than human- that made women and children your property...just like the 'good old days'! Well we've all got news for you- the 'good old days' weren't that great unless you were white and male and that ain't fair. Not to us and for damn sure not for our children!"

Duncan stared speechless at Gracie- not even sure it was really her. He turned on Fate again. "Witch! You and your kind have ruined America and you right here have ruined my beautiful sweet wife- look what you've turned her into!"

Fate spoke quietly and calmly, but it seemed to echo across the room, fill his head, and burn into his brain.

"No, Duncan. We helped. We've helped as we could individually when the laws changed and people were suffering because of it- not just the 'bad' people you all were trying to shut out of society, but your own people- when you were too filled with anger and ignorance to see it. We helped."

"Yes, we pooled our energies together and coordinated what happened to the government. But it never would've happened unless your women were fed up with how things were going. We didn't 'cast a spell' on an entire gender of Americans, you dumbass. That's not something we can do. This is."

And she smiled at him through her bruises and the blood drying on her lips.

He tried to move but he couldn't. He watched helpless and horrified as she shook out her hair, and dozens of scorpions dropped out of it; gold, silver and bronze, hitting the floor with soft little metallic 'plinks'.

The room was silent except for the sound of hundreds of arachnid toes and they circled his feet twice before running up his legs and disappearing into his nostrils and ears.

"See? Like that."

In retrospect, it probably wasn't the wisest thing she'd ever done but it was oh so satisfying to see the dark stain of urine blossom and grow on the front of his blue jeans.

She'd released him into Gracie's care, and he and Gracie had gone home- she to wash his jeans and boxer shorts before tending her own wounds and then making dinner for the kids.

They told the children mommy had fallen down a flight of stairs.

'Round about midnight, Fate was awakened by armed men surrounding her bed. She'd been taken into custody and formally charged with witchcraft and treason.

At the insistence of the preacher and every single man in the church, Duncan had been deputized and put in charge of the trial…such as it would be, since he had seen the witchcraft with his own eyes- making him the resident expert on witches.

He took this responsibility very seriously and delved into the internet for a crash course on 'How to Deal With Witches'.

Epilogue

If it weren't her own self standing toes-over the edge of the bridge, and if she weren't still so sore from the beating, she would've laughed out loud.

"You know, this doesn't make any sense at all, right? In fact, I'm pretty sure you're getting your information from an old comedy movie."

That the crowd closing in on her was holding pitchforks only made the scene even more surreal- who in this suburban area even owned a pitchfork? And yet, here they were- all bobbing up and down in a cheerfully macabre manner.

"Silence, witch!" the man right in front of her wearing a long black judge's robe spit out the word 'witch' contemptuously. "We've heard enough out of your kind!"

She tried again.

"Come on, Duncan. I'm not made of wood. Surely you of all people know that, right?" Fate managed a small ironic smile and winked at Duncan, barely concealing her hatred of him.

Duncan narrowed his eyes and backed away one step, lowering his pitchfork and pointing it directly at her chest. Slowly he raised it so one tine pushed her chin upwards, exposing her long soft neck.

Her hair a mass of waves in shades of gold, silver, and bronze- was clearly not made of wood.

She was still wearing only the scarlet satin bathrobe, and it accentuated her un-trunk-like body that was that luscious womanly combination of muscle and softness.

No, she was not made of wood.

Neither did she weigh the same as a duck, something they'd already ascertained by enlisting the aid of an exceptionally crabby and obese Muscovy drake who'd been minding his own business and taking a nap at the side of the river and who had glared and hissed through the entire indignity.

Nevertheless, Duncan had been ordered to try her as a witch with the understanding that she was not to get out of it alive.

So there they were.

Accidentally, their eyes met and locked.

Their entire brief and tumultuous history flashed between them for just an instant before Fate raised her eyebrow questioningly and Duncan lowered his eyes and turned away from her. His small and satisfied smile did not escape her notice.

"We all know the facts. If the accused is a witch, she'll float to the surface and be burned at the stake. If she's innocent, she'll sink to the bottom."

Fate shook her head in disbelief and disgust. There was no way in hell she was going to beg for mercy from this mob of unappreciative ignorant idiots.

"You're a disgusting little toad, you know that, Duncan?"

Before Duncan could order that she be pushed off the bridge, she jumped.

In the few moments it took for her to reach the water, she mentally forcibly severed the telepathic rope that connected her to Gracie, causing her more physical pain than anything she'd ever experienced, and making what was to come seem tame and anticlimactic.

The actual rope binding her ankles and wrists kept her slender body straight as an arrow and she hit the water vertically and cleanly, sinking below the surface with nary a splash.

Cold.

The water was fucking cold and almost immediately she began to shiver.

She gasped involuntarily and her lungs screamed out in protest at the icy water invading them.

Fate couldn't do anything but sink and think. The lyrics of a James Taylor song popped into her head.

'I know what it means to freeze to death, to lose a little life with every breath.
To say goodbye to life on earth and come around again,
Lord have mercy on the frozen man.'

To come around again.

Bodies come and bodies go- they are horribly fickle and perishable, but that spark within; the spark that takes a lump of carbon-based material and gives it life- the spark that religious people call a Soul- that is Energy.

And energy cannot be destroyed, only diverted.

As her lips and fingers and toes turned blue with cold and lack of oxygen, her retinas flashed fireworks the color of blood and fire, and her brain became frantic even as her body became heavy.

Tired. So tired, yet so afraid.

She felt the energy leaving her body behind and the last thought her mind received before giving into mortality was from Datura.

"Lord love a duck, girl! Focus! I didn't have time, but you do! I'll see you on the other side!"

And everything went black and silent.

The crowd stood on the bridge, eyes peeled to the surface of the water; watching with intense and edgy bloodthirsty anticipation.

When Fate had disappeared under the surface, a trail of bubbles had appeared- strong at first, then fading and intermittent, and then the water was still and smooth as glass.

Finally they all realized that they hadn't blinked in several minutes and as one they squeezed their eyes shut and sighed, exhaling the last vestiges of Black Orchid from their lungs.

"Well, Duncan- I guess she ain't a witch", someone murmured. "Hey- where'd Duncan go?" It was assumed that he'd left once she jumped- Duncan had always been queasy about the strangest things... and the crowd dissipated quietly.

No one noticed the disgruntled Muscovy on the bank of the river, or his companion with brown eyes flecked with green; eyes that were closed with exhaustion and bill wearily tucked under wing feathers that glittered from being waterlogged and ruffled from effort- feathers that shimmered in hues of gold, silver and bronze.

The reeds at the bank of the river rustled and parted right in front of her, and beady black eyes glared at her querulously.

Quick as a blink, the duck swallowed the toad, and then matter-of-factly re-tucked her bill under her wing to continue her nap.

www.ingramcontent.com/pod-product-compliance
Lightning Source LLC
Chambersburg PA
CBHW070838250626
47159CB00003B/827